THE FERRY MAN'S HOUSE

THE FERRYMAN'S TALES

CATHERINE POAG

◆ FriesenPress

Suite 300 - 990 Fort St
Victoria, BC, v8v 3K2
Canada

www.friesenpress.com

This book has no affiliation with The Rideau Regional Centre, all stories about the centre are made up from my own imagination.

This book is loosely based on the ghost story of the Rideau Ferry 'ferryman', but the rest of the story is made up of my own imagination.

Author Photo by John David Photography

ISBN
978-1-03-910013-8 (Hardcover)
978-1-03-910012-1 (Paperback)
978-1-03-910014-5 (eBook)

1. (Fiction, Thrillers, Suspense)

Distributed to the trade by The Ingram Book Company

Enjoy!

Doag

To the Parenting Committee.
Thank you for teaching me to follow my dreams.

Enjoy!

Good

TABLE OF CONTENTS

1

ARRIVING

JUNE 17, 1984

On a cold and rainy dark night, Jack Garrett Jr. stood at the Yellow Cottage dock's end. His wife, Margaret Garrett, was up in the kitchen, preparing the fish they'd caught earlier that day for supper. Dressed head to toe in bright yellow rain gear, Jack arranged their small wooden rowboat to set sail.

Jack Garrett was a tall man. He had dark brown hair, which had started to turn grey around his temples. His father used to own the ferry business, but Jack went against his family's wishes in continuing it and instead created his own minor maple-syrup business on the farm. He had always thought ill of his father's business, often making his wife worry.

The couple had one son, named Benjamin, whom Jack hoped would one day take over the new family business, but Benjamin had other plans. Benjamin had always had a knack for arguments, and his teachers often told him that he should become a lawyer. Since grade school, Benjamin had longed to get out of Rideau Ferry. He hoped to travel the world and only come back to visit his family. When Benjamin graduated from high school, he jetted off to England, with his high grades and family money, where he attended Oxford University for an undergrad in philosophy. He finished in two years instead of four, never taking a summer break. Once he completed his degree, he was accepted into Oxford's law program, where he learned how much he loved to fight against the justice system. His school performance was watched closely by his professors, giving him a step up on his classmates. When he graduated, the country's highest blue-collar law firms fought over who would employ him. Benjamin chose Asher and Associates, where he knew he could make the most money, giving him the chance to take his summers off to travel the world, and of course, visit his mother.

Margaret came out of the cottage, her head covered with a bonnet to save her hair from the rain. She tightly held her picnic basket with their supper as she walked down toward the dock. She knew the supper would not be eaten, but she had been unable to sit still all day; cooking soothed her anxiousness. Jack helped his wife settle smoothly into the boat and pushed them off. He dipped the oars into the icy water as Margaret lit her oil lamp for them to see ahead. Every so often, the couple had to bail out a bucket of water from the driving rain. The two wanted to turn around, but they knew they needed to tie up their last loose end.

The water was getting rougher by the minute. As the tip of the ferry poked through the fog, Jack rowed harder through the rough water. Jack could see the worried look on Margaret's fair visage as they got closer to their destination. Jack knew his wife had never accepted how he handled things—he had watched her pace the floor all day. Jack had tried to convince Margaret to stay home, but she decided she could not let him go alone. He knew that the closer they got, the more worried she became.

Margaret Garrett was a short woman with long, silky brown hair she often wore in a bun. She spent a lot of her time in the kitchen, the garden, and when Benjamin was young, homeschooling him. Margaret's family, unlike Jack's, was poor. Margaret grew up on a small farm in Lombardy with five sisters. Her father worked as a coal miner, often being away from home for months at a time, sending back everything he made to Margaret's mother to feed and clothe their six girls.

At a young age, Margaret became a housemaid for a rich family in the next town over; there, she cooked and cleaned for her room and board. For a while, she was happy; the family had a young boy around her age whom she would spend time with when she was not cooking or cleaning. The young boy's name was Jack Garrett, who would later become her husband. The two spent more and more time together, until one day, Jack asked Margaret to run away with him. He knew a cottage on Miller's Bay where they could live and raise a family. Jack wanted to start his own business rather than taking over his father's. Margaret accepted, and they left that night. They never looked back—until today.

They pulled up to Rideau Ferry's shore, and Margaret wrapped her shawl around her as the temperature dipped. They struggled out of the boat as it swung forward because of the waves and hit the shore. Jack grabbed the bow line and pulled the boat up onto the shore so the waves couldn't take it away. A big gust of wind came and blew out their lamp. Jack fumbled to light it again. Once he had, they climbed the shoreline to the house at the top of the hill.

. . .

In Ottawa, Elizabeth had just gotten off her plane from Paris and saw a man holding a small white sign with her name across it. She walked toward the man, whom she presumed was a taxi driver, and politely smiled as she gave him her bag.

"Hello, Ms. Harland. My name's Charlie. Your grandparents have arranged for me to take you to their home in Rideau Ferry. How was your flight? I notice it was delayed a bit. Was everything okay?"

"Hello, Charlie, thank you," Elizabeth said as she handed her bags to him. "My flight was good." She was headed an hour west to visit her grandparents in their modest town of Rideau Ferry.

Meanwhile, as Elizabeth got into the taxi, across the little airport, Benjamin Garrett had just arrived from England. He was a high-class defence attorney just a few years out of law school and was visiting his parents for the summer.

Elizabeth's taxi driver quickly glanced down at his watch and read the time. It was 6:47. They were still fifteen minutes from the ferry. He pressed harder on the gas pedal and tried to speed up their trip to make the last ferry.

The ferry master, Luther Neville, was a crotchety old man who did not like many people. He was tall, slender, and well-dressed. Luther had taken the ferry over from Jack's father and ran the ferry just how Mr. Garrett used to, from nine in the morning to seven at night. If you were not back for the last ferry ride at seven, you were stuck, following rules Mr. Garrett had put in place himself. Like Mr. Garrett, Luther often offered people a place to stay if they did not make the ferry in time.

Elizabeth's taxi finally pulled up to the ferry dock.

7:01 p.m.

The driver jumped out of the car and told Elizabeth to quickly grab her things as they ran to the ferry, but they were too late. The ferry had pushed off and started drifting away on its last ride across the lake.

A small red Chevy Bel Air drew up beside them; then Benjamin sprang out and ran toward the ferry, hoping it might turn around. He slowed to a stroll, stopping before Luther Garrett at the end of the dock, who had just helped push off the last ferry of the night.

Elizabeth had said goodbye to her taxi driver, Charlie, and made her way down to the docks to talk with Luther about staying the night until she could cross over to get to her grandparents' house.

"Hello, Luther, it's been a while," Benjamin started.

Luther chuckled and said, "Benjamin Garrett . . . you're back, and I see you've brought a girl."

"Oh, you're mistaken," Elizabeth interrupted. "My name is Elizabeth Harland. I'm in town visiting my grandparents."

"Luther, this poor girl needs to get over to her grandparents. They'll be worried." Benjamin pulled out his wallet and started to take out a twenty-dollar bill. "Help me, and help her out. I'll make it worth your while."

"No, you cannot bribe me. You know my rules, young man. The rules have been around since you were a wee boy. You and the pretty lady can stay with me tonight," Luther spat back.

Benjamin wearily accepted.

Elizabeth raised her hand to Luther's. "Thank you, Mr. Neville."

"Luther will be fine."

Luther invited the two young people into his home and gestured them to sit on one of the four chairs in a circle in the living room. He left the room, telling them he would make a pot of tea.

Benjamin introduced himself to Elizabeth. "Hey, I'm Benjamin Garrett."

"Hi, I'm Elizabeth Harland," Elizabeth replied shyly.

"Oh, are you related to the Harlands who own the Rideau Ferry store? When I was young, my friends and I would always boat there for ice-cream."

"Yeah, those are my grandparents." Elizabeth nodded as she spoke.

Then the two sat in dead silence, for neither of them knew what to say next. They stared forward, trying not to glance at each other and make the silence worse. The two had little in common. Elizabeth was a small girl, blonde, pretty, just eighteen and unsure of what she wanted to do with her life. Benjamin was tall, brunet, handsome, twenty-five years of age, and a successful lawyer.

Elizabeth got up suddenly, catching Benjamin off guard. Politely, she said, "I'll see if Luther needs help." With that, she headed to the kitchen. Benjamin remained where he was, his gaze wandering around the dim room. The room had a floor lamp in the corner, which gave off little light, and a layer of dust filled the room. The room seemed barely touched and had clearly not been lived in for quite some time. Off to the corner of the room was a large picture window, surrounded by dark red curtains pulled up to the sides. Next to it, Luther had an old wooden Windsor rocking chair. It was angled perfectly to look out the window at the lake.

As Benjamin made his way toward the window facing the lake, Elizabeth appeared from the kitchen handing him a cup of tea from Mr. Garrett and disappeared again into the kitchen. Benjamin had a sip of his tea and took a seat in the large rocking chair. He peered out the window and saw a small wooden rowboat pulled onto the shore. He imagined the great times he'd had with his parents on their family rowboat, but he was snapped out of his daydream by a scream.

He ran to the kitchen and busted open the kitchen door to find his father, Jack, on the floor in a pool of blood, completely still. He looked around the kitchen for Elizabeth and saw a blood trail leading out the door and another that led up the stairs. He hurried to his father's side and knelt to check his pulse. He started to cry when he knew his father was gone. He knew the ferry man had done this—he had heard rumours of things that went on in this house, the stories of missing people.

He snapped out of his thoughts as he quickly looked around the room for Elizabeth. She screamed again from upstairs. He turned and ran up the stairs, but a large, strong man grabbed him and put something over his face. The next thing Benjamin saw was darkness.

2
The Dress

BENJAMIN WAS JOLTED awake by someone grabbing his arm. He opened his eyes to see Elizabeth peering over him, blood all over her short white dress. He tried to sit up in the bed, but everything hurt. Elizabeth reached for his back and helped him sit upright as Benjamin struggled to remember what he had seen the previous night.

"What happened last night?" Benjamin asked Elizabeth.

"When I went into the kitchen to help Luther, there was a man lying on the floor, and Luther was covered in blood, so I ran upstairs, and he chased after me."

"Did he try to explain what had happened?"

"No, he heard you rush into the kitchen, so he went downstairs. I screamed to warn you, as I tried to open the window to escape, but it was locked, and I couldn't find a key. I tried to run out of the bedroom and go down, but that's when Luther met me at the door. You were in his arms, and he set you on the bed. I tried to wake you, but I think he drugged you," Elizabeth explained.

"What are we going to do?" Benjamin asked.

"I think the only way to get out of here alive will be to follow his rules," Elizabeth said with a saddened smile.

The doorknob on the door before them started to turn as the door was pushed open and Luther appeared.

Benjamin had a sudden rush of energy as he continued to think about his dad. He tried to jump to his feet to attack Luther, but immediately discovered he was too weak to do so, falling back into the bed. Whatever he had been drugged with the previous night was still affecting him.

Luther helped Benjamin stand and then put him in a small chair that seemed almost meant for a child—it seemed to be a child's bedroom—and served him some breakfast. Benjamin stayed put as he tried to get some food into him.

Next, Luther turned to Elizabeth. "Follow me." They headed into another bedroom, where Luther handed Elizabeth a clean dress that he had taken from the closet. "Get changed right away and meet me downstairs for breakfast."

Elizabeth nodded with a sad, paltry smile as Luther headed back down the grand staircase.

Elizabeth quickly put on the dress Luther had given to her. The dress was a short white and red striped dress with a white apron. It looked like a hospital candy-striper dress.

She smiled to herself and remembered her mother wearing the same style of dress when working at the hospital. Once Elizabeth was dressed, she rushed down the staircase and into the kitchen. The bloody mess that she had seen in Luther's kitchen the previous night was no longer there. Hope flickered within her, and she secretly pinched herself to see if it was all a trick or maybe a dream.

She looked up to see Luther standing there with a big smile on his face and a cup of coffee in his hands as he gestured for her to sit down at the small kitchen table. She pulled out a chair and took a seat. Luther set a cup of coffee and a plate full of toast, eggs, bacon, and home fries in front of her. She nodded as a thank you, picking up the fork as she took a sip of her coffee.

Luther turned to her, pulled out a seat at the table, and sat down. "Do you wonder why you saw what you saw last night?"

Elizabeth quickly nodded and realized her hope was gone. This was not a dream or a trick; it was a nightmare.

Elizabeth had heard the rumours of the ferry man. She knew if she ever wanted to see her grandparents, Emily and Frank Harland, again, she would listen to what Luther had to say.

He looked to her with a crooked yellow smile and said, "Well, Elizabeth, let me tell you a story . . ."

3
Mr. Garrett

MY PARENTS GOT married on December 19, 1936. They were already pregnant with a baby boy: me. My mother gave birth to me on September 10, 1937, and I grew up in a small house on the edge of town.

We had very little money, but my parents did what they could to keep me well fed and clothed. My father worked as a cobbler, and my mom stayed home with my three younger brothers and me.

When I reached the age of twelve, I got my first job at a little store in Rideau Ferry: your grandparents' store. I learned a lot from your grandparents. They treated me like their son, feeding me lunch every day and buying me Christmas and birthday gifts.

Your grandfather, Mr. Harland, told me stories about the ferry man who lived across the street. His name was Jack Garrett, Senior. He was Benjamin Garrett's grandfather, but your friend Benjamin does not know that.

The stories Mr. Harland told me would terrify me as I walked by the ferry man every day on my way to work. Many people said that the ferry man killed people who did not make the last ferry. They would have to stay the night with Mr. Garrett, for there was no hotel in our small town, and many said that the people who went into his house for the night never came back out. These people were often in a rush to get across, so they would accept the offer to stay.

The rumours first started when a family who stayed overnight at his house were never seen again. Mr. Garrett told the police that the family decided to move away and had left very early in the morning, before anyone was awake.

One night, when I was just about to leave the store and head home, Mr. Garrett stopped me.

"Good evening, young man," Mr. Garrett greeted me.

"Hello," I politely said.

"Aren't you the boy who works for the Harlands?"

"Yes, I am."

"I've always wanted to know more about the Harlands. Our families used to be close. Would you like to come in for a cup of tea?"

I was unsure what to say. Mr. Harland had always warned me to avoid Mr. Garrett, but curiosity had taken over me, and I accepted.

I followed Mr. Garrett into his house. A tall, slender man, he wore a black coat and cap, which he hung on a coat rack as we entered through his door. As I stepped inside, he took my overcoat and hung it beside his. He told me to take a seat in the living room as he made a pot of tea.

I sat down in the living room and surveyed my surroundings. He had a small fireplace with a big fire, and all the paintings in the room were red. They sent chills down my spine, for it seemed like they were from a mental institution. None seemed to picture anything—they were all just differently shaped red blotches. It reminded me of the drawings doctors would have you look at to determine what was happening in your head.

I got lost in my thoughts, and then I heard footsteps coming, so I turned to see Mr. Garrett in the doorway. He had two cups of tea on a platter with a small pitcher of cream and a matching bowl of sugar cubes.

He sat down next to me with a smile and handed me my cup. I put two sugar cubes in it and a bit of cream, then took a long sip. He did the same and set down his cup. He looked at me as if he were waiting for me to speak. We sat in silence for a few moments.

"Why did you accept my offer for tea? Have you not heard the stories from the locals about me?" Mr. Garrett spoke, cutting the silence.

I sat there and pondered his question. Why had I come in? Mr. Harland had warned me about Mr. Garrett. I looked up at Mr. Garrett as he stared down at me. I knew I had to reply, but before I could, he spoke again.

"Will you tell me what is happening in town? I am very lonely here, for no one will talk with me."

I gazed over to the far side of the room to ponder his question. I figured that it would not kill me to clue him in a bit, so I started to explain what had been happening in the town.

"Well, the Harlands' country store has been very busy. They started selling homemade baked goods that Mrs. Harland makes, and everyone in town is buying them as quickly as she gets them on the shelf. I have learned that Mr. Peters comes in every Wednesday at exactly three o'clock to buy a can of pop and a package of cigarettes, and Miss Charlotte comes in every three days to buy baby food. I keep telling her to buy more at one time, but she says her baby keeps changing what he likes."

We talked until ten o'clock at night.

I looked across the room at the grandfather clock, which read 10:01. "I must get going, since I don't want my parents to worry," I explained to him.

"Oh, yes, you should get going," he started, "but maybe you could come back tomorrow and chat some more."

"Yes, I guess I could come back," I said as he walked me to the door.

He handed me my overcoat off the coat rack and pulled the door open for me. "Goodbye, son. See you tomorrow," he said as I stepped onto the gravel and headed on my way.

The next day, I did the same thing. I went to work, and as soon as I was finished my work for the day, I took Mr. Garrett's last ferry with him, as I lived across the lake.

"Good evening, Mr. Garrett," I said as I climbed on board.

"Hello, Luther, how was the store today?"

"We had a very slow day. Very few people out and about with the rainy weather."

"Are you coming in for tea tonight?" Mr. Garrett asked me.

"Yes, but only for an hour. My mom wants me home for dinner."

For four weeks, I went to Mr. Garrett's house every night after work for an hour before dinner. At the end of our conversation one night, Mr. Garrett turned to me and said, "Are you interested in learning how I run the ferry?"

Since I was a young boy, I had always been interested in boats and planes and had always wanted to know how they worked. I had also become very interested in Mr. Garrett's life. After getting to know him, I started to forget about the nasty rumours about him. He seemed so much nicer than people said.

"Yes, I would love to," I replied.

"Great," he started. "Ask Mr. Harland at work tomorrow if you can have a few mornings off in two weeks. That should be enough notice to get it off from the store."

"Thank you!" I jumped in excitement. "I will see you in two weeks!" I yelled as I ran off toward my house, for I had taken the ferry with Mr. Garrett to his house, which was three blocks from mine.

I was so excited that I ran to the store the next morning to ask if I could have that day off, but my happiness was soon squashed when Mr. Harland said no. He explained that I could not be seen with Mr. Garrett again, or I would lose my job. I took my job very seriously, and since my family was very poor, I could not afford to lose it.

Rideau Ferry was a small town. Everybody knew everybody, and many people enjoyed the art of gossip; therefore, I never went to see Mr. Garrett again until years later when my family and I had to take the ferry over the water.

We were too late that evening, and we missed the ferry. Mr. Garrett invited myself and my family into the house and told us to wait in the living room while he made tea. I looked toward my mom, who had an uneasy look on her face. She was one of the many who believed the rumours about Mr. Garrett, but she knew we did not have the money to go back to Perth and find somewhere else to stay. Moments later, Mr. Garrett came into the room with a pot of tea and enough cups for my mother, father, myself, and my three younger brothers.

I had just turned sixteen years old; my middle brother was twelve, and my younger brothers, the twins, were ten years old. They both were very short and fat, with blondish hair and crystal blue eyes; they looked nothing like myself or my father. My father was a large man, very tall and burly, with what used to be brown hair, which had started to turn grey in recent years.

"Would you like some tea?" Mr. Garrett asked my mother.

"Yes, please," she said politely.

Mr. Garrett poured her tea and handed it to her. My mother grabbed it and placed her long, thin fingers around the porcelain cup. My mother was a tall woman who always looked tired but always had a smile on her face. She was very thin and had long brown hair.

Mr. Garrett continued to pour tea and set a cup in front of each of us.

"Thank you," I said to him as he set mine in front of me.

As we sat around Mr. Garrett's living room and drank our tea, the paintings on the wall again caught my eye.

Mr. Garrett saw this and asked, "Do you want to know where they are from?"

I shyly nodded.

"Well, I got them from the Rideau Regional Hospital in Smiths Falls."

I did not know how to feel then, seeing that I had been correct in my assumptions. I wanted to inquire how he got them, but I was soon interrupted by my mother telling myself and my three brothers, Walter, Aaron, and Joseph, that it was time for bed.

Mr. Garrett quickly got up and showed us to our rooms, which left our parents in the living room. Our room had four small beds, one next to the other, with small bedside tables between them. He had laid out pyjamas for us on each of the beds; it seemed he had a closet full of clothes for every age.

Mr. Garrett left the room as we hastily dressed. He returned moments later with extra blankets. He put one at the end of each bed and then tucked us in, shut off the light, and closed the door behind him. I heard a small click, almost the sound of a door being locked, but I was too comfortable at the time to realize. I figured I had probably imagined it.

Now, when I think about this story, I wish I had gotten up and checked. I drifted into a deep sleep, only to be awakened by a high-pitched scream coming from downstairs. But I was so tired that I somehow went right back to sleep. I now wonder what was in the tea we had been served.

I was woken up that morning by the smell of breakfast downstairs. I sat up and looked around the room to see my three brothers gone from their beds. They usually got up before I did, so I shrugged it off. The beds were neatly made, and there was a small pile at the end of my bed. I curiously got out of bed and picked up the pile; it was a new change of clothes for the day. Mr. Garrett must have brought it up when I was asleep. I had not heard him come in, but I had been exhausted. I thought about the scream I had heard, but I quickly pushed it out of my mind, telling myself it was just a nightmare.

I promptly changed and headed down the large staircase and made my way into the kitchen.

Mr. Garrett told me to sit at his small table in the corner of the room. I looked around the room for my brothers and my parents, but they were nowhere to be seen. I turned to Mr. Garrett to ask where they were, but I was interrupted by a lovely breakfast put in front of me: eggs, bacon, toast, home fries, and a cup of coffee.

"Eat up, or else it will get cold," Mr. Garrett said.

"Why aren't my parents and brothers eating with us? Have they already eaten?"

"I didn't want to be the one to tell you this, but your parents left in the middle of the night."

I looked at him with disbelief. "Where did they go? We have no money. Where are my brothers?" I yelled.

"They took your brothers with them."

"Why didn't they take me?" I started to sob. "Where did they go?"

"They wouldn't tell me," Mr. Garrett said smoothly.

I stood up, pushing away the food before me, and ran toward the door.

"No, you can't go!" Mr. Garrett yelled as he grabbed my arm.

I struggled with him as I screamed, "Let me go! I need to find my parents!"

"They don't want you anymore!" Mr. Garrett yelled back.

I fell back into my chair and started to sob. "Why?"

"They can't afford it; it's time for you to live on your own."

"I can't live on my own," I said between the sobs.

"You can live with me," Mr. Garrett said with a smirk.

"I can?" My sobs turned to tears rolling down my cheeks.

"Yes, I can take care of you. You'll never have to worry about money again."

"I won't?"

"Yes, I will take care of you as if you were my own," Mr. Garrett said with a smile.

"Okay," I said as my final tear dripped down my face.

For the first few weeks, Mr. Garrett kept me inside. He said I needed to be sheltered from the reporters' and the police's questions. I later found out that no one noticed my family was gone for a few weeks.

"Can I go over to the Harlands' country store to let Mr. Harland know I am alright?" I asked shyly, already knowing the answer.

"No, you need to stay inside. Who knows what you might say outside the house to the police or reporters?"

"What I might say? My parents just ran away."

"They will try to convince you otherwise; it is best to stay inside."

I knew not to try changing his mind; I knew he wanted me to stay inside, but I did not know if it was for my safety or his.

I found out later that the police and townspeople had not even realized we were missing. Mr. Harland assumed I had chosen the ferry man over my job at the store and brushed it off, and my father's work had thought he had taken ill. It had taken one person three more weeks to start asking questions about where our family might have gone.

Some thought we had gone to the next town over for better jobs, while others thought we were just at home because one of us was very sick. Some thought our family had been murdered, and some thought we had been kidnapped.

One morning, I was sitting in the living room, and I heard a loud banging at the door, followed by a man's voice.

"Mr. Garrett, open up. It's the police; we have a few questions for you."

Mr. Garrett waltzed into the living room and calmly said, "Please go make a pot of tea for our guests and then go up to your room."

I nodded and went through the door to the kitchen. I put water in the kettle and turned it on as I pulled out the teapot and put in two tea bags. As I waited for the kettle to boil, I tiptoed over to the door and put my ear against it.

"Hello, gentlemen. Do come in," I heard Mr. Garrett say. "What can I do for you today?"

"We have heard that the missing Neville family was last seen going into your house on the night of the twenty-first. Do you know where they went?" the first voice asked.

"Ahh yes, I remember the family quite well, very nice family," Mr. Garrett replied.

"Where are they now?" the second voice asked.

"I am not sure," Mr. Garrett replied.

"Where did they go?" the first police officer asked again.

"I have not a clue. I don't keep track of each family who rides my ferry or who doesn't make the ferry in time."

"Did they stay the night at your home, if they missed the ferry?" the second police officer asked.

"Isn't your big fundraiser for the year coming up?" Mr. Garrett questioned.

"Yes, sir, we're trying to buy new uniforms for the men."

"Well, let me go get my cheque book," Mr. Garrett said as he got up from his seat.

"Thank you, sir," the second police officer said.

I heard Mr. Garrett's footsteps move closer toward the kitchen, and I fumbled to turn around and run up the stairs toward my room. I didn't understand why Mr. Garrett did not want me to be in the room, or why he would not answer their questions. I watched out my window at the front door as Mr. Garrett handed the officers a cheque, and they headed on their way. I heard the door close again, and Mr. Garrett called me down to the living room.

"Who was that?" I asked, to see if he would tell me.

"Just the police asking some questions, telling me I made the right choice keeping you inside," he answered calmly.

It was at that moment that I started to become suspicious about what Mr. Garrett was doing. I wondered what else he had been lying about. From what I knew so far about Mr. Garrett, I knew he always got what he wanted; he would throw money at his problems. I knew the only way to figure out what he was doing was to go along with what he wanted and just observe.

I spent a very long time indoors, so much so that my skin started to look translucent. I sat in a wooden rocking chair most of my days, looking out a big window and onto the lake. Mr. Garrett bought me lots of books to read and paint supplies to occupy my time. I got into a routine. Every morning, I would wake up to Mr. Garret, who would knock on my door at seven in the morning.

I would enjoy breakfast with him until he went to run the ferry. I spent my mornings by the fireplace, where I would read or write in my journal. Around noon, Mr. Garrett would come back home to make us sandwiches. He went back to the ferry an hour later, and I would spend the afternoon painting pictures on my easel set up in front of the big window that faced the lake.

He would return home in the evening, and the two of us would make dinner together. I saw him as a father figure. He fed me, clothed me, entertained me. I almost did not miss my old family, since Mr. Garrett treated me much better: He fed me my favourite meals, bought me clothes, and gave me a lot of books.

Each evening we would sit in the living room, and Mr. Garrett would tell me stories about who he saw on the ferry that day and where they were headed. He talked until I had to go to bed each night at nine. Mr. Garrett would tuck me in but always bring me up a book to read, in case I could not fall asleep right away.

I loved our routine, but it all went away when, one evening, Mr. Garrett came home an hour early and handed me different clothes than I usually wore. He told me to go change, and I obeyed. Too frightened to ask why, I went upstairs and put on the tan corduroy slacks he had given me and a blue pullover sweater.

After I was dressed, I went back downstairs to see Mr. Garrett, who had also changed into dressy black pants and a sports coat. He handed me my black dress jacket and black dress boots. I quickly put them on and followed him out the door.

4

The Hospital

LUTHER STOPPED HIS story to ask Elizabeth if she was finished with her breakfast. She nodded, and he cleaned up her plate. He placed the food from the table into the icebox. Luther refilled his own coffee mug and Elizabeth's and asked her if she wanted him to continue the story.

Elizabeth, who was scared but curious to hear what happened next, quickly said, "Yes, sir, but what about Benjamin?"

"He is very tired, and he already knows this part of the story," Mr. Neville explained.

"How?" Elizabeth pushed.

"Just wait and see," Mr. Neville firmly said as he started his story again.

. . .

Mr. Garrett opened the passenger-side door of his small car and gestured for me to climb inside. Once I was seated, he shut the door, hurried to the driver's side, and got in. He started the car and pulled away.

I looked around the car to see an old, brown-leather carpet bag packed in the backseat. I turned to Mr. Garrett and asked, frightened, "Where are we headed?"

He answered me with a pat on the knee and a small, sad smile. I started to get worried. It must be somewhere bad if he would not tell me where we were going.

We drove for about twenty minutes before we hit the next town over from us. This town was called Smiths Falls; it was a bit bigger than our little town of Rideau Ferry. Smiths Falls had many more stores and had a good-sized hospital.

Mr. Garrett finally turned into a long driveway with trees all down the sides. As we drove, I saw a large building with a sign that read, "Welcome to Rideau Regional Hospital."

Mr. Garrett pulled up to the front of the building, then swiftly got out of the car and retrieved the carpet bag from the back seat. "Hurry up. Follow behind me."

We were greeted at the door by two male nurses in white uniforms. They both smiled sincerely at me while they took the bag from Mr. Garret and told us to follow them.

The two nurses took us down a long, bright hallway. It felt like we had been walking forever by the time we turned into the west wing, where we were greeted by a female nurse who looked to be a couple years older than me. She was very short and thin, wearing a white and red striped dress with a white apron. She nodded to the men in white, and they gave her the bag. "Come with me, please," she said to me.

"What is going on?" I asked in confusion.

Mr. Garrett pulled me into a hug and said, "I can no longer take care of you the way that you should be taken care of. They'll take great care of you here."

"But I love living with you. I don't need to be taken care of. I can take care of myself," I pleaded.

He gave me a small nod and a smile as a tear ran down his face. Then he turned and followed the men in white out of the wing and back down the hallway, leaving me with the nurse in red and white.

"You will be safer in here," she said. "Follow me. I'll show you your room."

Safer here? I thought. *I was safe with Mr. Garrett.* I quickly followed and tried to keep up with her fast pace. *My room? The only room that was mine was back in Rideau Ferry.*

We entered a room with B26 written on the plaque nailed to the front. The walls of the little room were painted white, and it had a bed in the corner. Next to it was a bedside table with a short lamp and a window in the middle. On the other side of the room were a dresser, a small desk, and a chair.

The nurse set the bag on my chair as she unpacked it, put the clothes in the dresser, and set my journal and some books on my desk.

"I'll be right back," she said as she left the room. She came back with new clothes for me to change into to match the other patients.

"Please, put these on, and I'll go get the rest of the paperwork I need to have you fill out." She handed me the clothing as she left the room.

I put on the clothes she'd brought me. It was a pair of blue slacks and a blue short-sleeved top, white canvas shoes, and a black button-up sweater for when I was cold. I put my old clothes in my dresser, sat on the edge of my bed, and waited for the nurse to come back.

It was then that it finally sank in: Mr. Garrett had left me in at the Rideau Regional Hospital. From my time at the country store, I knew it was a mental institution.

When Mr. Garrett admitted me to the hospital, I was just sixteen and had grown to the height of five-foot nine. I was quite thin, with little muscle, so I was frail and weak.

The small nurse came back into the room with a clipboard. She turned my desk chair around to face me and took a seat.

"Hello, Luther. My name is Nurse Darcy, and I'm going to ask you a few routine questions. Mr. Garrett filled most of the forms out, so I'll just make sure that what he filled out is correct."

I nodded in response.

"Full name is Luther Neville?"

"Yes," I replied.

She nodded and moved on to the next question. "Age sixteen?"

"Sixteen, yes."

"Any medical issues?"

"No."

"Birthdate?"

"September 10, 1937."

"Alright, I think I have everything we need for right now. You're free to go to dinner," she told me.

Another nurse, who was much older than Darcy, knocked on the door and entered the room. "Hello, Luther. My name is Anne," the older nurse said. "Follow me to the dining room now." She was stern and walked fast. I gathered that this was the nurse in charge.

I followed her into a huge dining room. She guided me to a seat at a table with five other boys who appeared around my age.

"Hello," I said to the boys.

I sat at the table, and she buckled me into my chair.

I looked at her with hurt and surprise in my eyes. "Why are you doing that?" I asked.

"It's protocol that we do this with every new patient until we know how they behave at mealtime," she answered with a snarl.

I slowly nodded as I tried to make sense of this all. *Why did Mr. Garrett bring me here? And what did I do wrong?* We sat in silence until trays of food were set in front of us. Each tray had a glass of milk, a glass a water, a bowl of tomato soup, a ham and cheese sandwich, and some red Jell-O for dessert. I tried to focus on my meal, as none of the boys spoke a word throughout the entire supper. As soon as I had finished my meal, Nurse Darcy came and unbuckled me.

I got up and followed her to my room. "Where have my things gone?"

"I took out your journal and put it in your desk drawer. As for your clothes, I put them away in storage. You can get them back when you leave," she said as she walked out the door. It was obvious that she did not have time for my questions.

I sat down at my desk, opened my journal, and printed the date in the top right-hand corner: June 19, 1953. I had just started to write when a boy who looked around my age rushed into my room, interrupting me.

"Hi!" the boy said.

I must have looked startled, because he told me his name as soon as he saw my face. "I'm Louis Harland."

"Hi, I'm Luther."

"Some of the other boys and I are going to go play cards in the games room. Would you like to come?"

I nodded quickly. At the time, I thought that I needed to make friends with someone since I didn't know how long I'd be there for, and I didn't know when Mr. Garrett was coming back for me—or if he ever would.

I shut my journal and put it in the drawer under my desk, then followed him out of the room and down the hall into what I guessed was the games room. It was a large room with about ten tables set up with chairs around them and a pile of board games on a shelf in the corner near the window.

We walked up to the table with four boys sitting around it. Louis took a seat and gestured for me to sit beside him. He introduced me to the young men at the table, who all nodded as their names were offered.

"Luther, I want you to meet the boys. That's Max Delbert. Beside him, Silas Axton. Next to him, Andrew Hadley, and then there at the end is Gabe Thurmond. Boys, here's Luther Neville."

I waved. Max shuffled the cards and dealt us each five cards as he explained the rules to me. We played the first game slowly so I would learn and sped up the next one. We played for quite a while, and at ten o'clock on the dot, Nurse Anne came in.

"Good evening, boys, it is curfew and time to return to your rooms," she told us.

We all got up, pushed in our chairs, and followed her down the hallway.

"Good night," I said to my new friends as we all entered our separate rooms.

I opened my top dresser drawer to look for my pyjamas that Mr. Garrett had packed for me only to find that all my clothes had been replaced by clothes given to me by the hospital. I changed into the hospital pyjamas, which were long blue and white striped bottoms with a button-up long-sleeved top. I climbed into my neatly made bed and drifted off to sleep.

In the middle of the night, I woke up to a loud crash coming from outside my room.

Max Delbert barged into my room. "Hey, Luther, get up!" he yelled.

"What's going on?" I questioned.

"Just come. It'll be fun."

I did as I was told and followed him out the door.

We rushed down the hallway. When we got to the main hallway, we were met by the other four boys, also in their hospital pyjamas. The mystery of what we were doing heightened, becoming more exciting as they took off running down the hallway. I sprinted and followed quickly behind.

We ran until we hit the dining hall, and the lead boy, Andrew Hadley, took us to the back of the dining hall and through the kitchen doors. We walked through the kitchen until we hit the back doors. I saw a male nurse coming toward us, and I began to turn around to run the other way when Max grabbed me and told me, "It's okay. We know him. He helps us out by smuggling things in here."

"Why does he do that?" I asked. "Won't he lose his job?"

"We found out he's in a relationship with a patient, so now he'll do whatever we want, as long as we don't tell," Max explained.

I gave him a nervous nod, and the male nurse was close enough for me to read his name tag, which read, "Mervyn." He nodded to me in acknowledgement—he knew I was new—and handed Andrew a cloth bag, then headed on his way.

Andrew told me to follow them, so I did, moving to the other side of the kitchen and then down a set of stairs into the basement. We went down a long hallway and into a small room set up with six Victorian-style, yellow-cushioned chairs that circled a rectangular wooden table. We each took a seat, and Andrew dumped the contexts of the bag out onto the table. Inside was a pack of cigarettes, a lighter, six chocolate bars, a deck of cards, and some poker chips.

Silas handed me a cigarette and a chocolate bar as Gabe shuffled the cards and Andrew passed out the poker chips. Gabe dealt the cards with a lit cigarette in his mouth and explained the game to me.

Silas taught me how to light the cigarette. I put it to my mouth and took a drag, which was followed by a cough. The boys laughed and told me that I would get used to it after a while.

Again, we played the first round slowly. I caught on quite quickly. We sat around until all hours of the night, playing poker, smoking, and eating chocolate. Once one in the morning hit, we cleaned up our poker game. I had not spoken much that night, for I didn't know what to say, but once we were finished cleaning up, I asked, "So, how come you guys are in here?"

Louis Harland spoke up first. "Well, Luther," he said, "my life back home wasn't great. My mother and father were murdered when I was thirteen years old, so a man by the name of Jack Garrett took me in. My life was good for a while; we had a schedule, but one day he brought me here. Sometimes he comes to visit but not often. I've tried to ask him why he brought me here, but he never answers my question. He always tells me it was for my own good, and that I will have a better life here."

I looked at him, *dumbfounded*. I could not believe what I had heard. He was brought here by Mr. Garrett too. He lived with him as well, and his parents disappeared too. I started thinking about the night my parents left with my brothers. I had never really considered that maybe something bad had happened. Had they been murdered too? So many thoughts were in my head that night. I suddenly felt very faint. *Did Mr. Garrett murder my parents?* My head got very fuzzy. Then there was black.

5

Answers

LUTHER STOPPED HIS story when he saw the light go out of Elizabeth's eyes. A worried expression came onto her face when she said, "Louis Harland, why does he have the same last name as me?"

Luther looked at her with sad eyes, "Well, dear, the Louis Harland in my story is, in fact, related to you—closely related."

Elizabeth gave him a puzzled look and replied, "You mean like an uncle? But my grandparents weren't murdered. They're alive."

"Yes, dear. Emily and Frank are alive. Let me finish my story, and then you'll understand," Luther said, his pointer finger touching his middle eye as if he were telling her that he knew all the town's secrets.

. . .

I woke up that next morning in my bed. I sat up quickly to find Nurse Darcy was in my room checking my vitals, her hand on my wrist to check my pulse.

"I'm so sorry for sneaking out last night," I apologized.

She rushed to the door and closed it. "Lower your voice!" she exclaimed.

I looked at her, confused.

"I don't think you boys deserve to be locked in your rooms. I don't believe that you boys deserve to be here. You are all good boys, so I keep their secret of sneaking out."

She pulled out my desk chair, turned it to face me, and took a seat. She took out her clipboard and asked, "How do you feel after you fainted last night?"

"I'm feeling better. Just a little hungry, I guess," I answered.

She nodded and wrote some things down on her clipboard before she ripped the piece of paper off, folded it up, and handed it to me.

"Alright, hurry up and get dressed, and then you can go to breakfast."

I got up from my bed and made it neatly. Then I got into a new blue uniform, and pulled on my sweater and my laceless, white-canvas shoes. Nurse Darcy told me the lack of laces was for "the patients' safety." I slipped her note into my pocket and rushed to breakfast.

I entered the dining hall, and Nurse Anne escorted me to a different table, a table with the five boys from the night before. She walked away without buckling me up, and I called after her to remind her, trying to keep on her good side. She just smiled and kept walking. The boys bombarded me with questions. They asked if I was alright or if I'd gotten in trouble that morning.

"What did Nurse Darcy say this morning when you woke up?" Max asked first.

"She said that she thought we deserved to be allowed to do what we want."

We were served breakfast with a tray of two pancakes, syrup, fruit, and orange juice. After, we chatted about the new board games that had been donated and about the many activities that were planned throughout that day. Andrew read out the activity board to us for the day. Listed on the board was "swimming or bowling in the morning, then family visiting hours in the afternoon."

We decided as a group we would go for a swim that day, so as soon as we were finished breakfast, we said our goodbyes and told each other we would meet at the pool.

I headed back down the long hallway to my room and opened my door to walk over to my dresser. I pulled out the last drawer and hoped that Nurse Darcy had put a swimming suit in there for me. Finally, finding myself blue swim shorts, I got changed, put Nurse Darcy's note inside my journal in my desk drawer, deciding I would read it later, and headed down toward the pool area.

The hospital was so huge that it was hard not to get lost in there, but I managed to get to the pool with little help. The boys and I swam all morning. We played Marco Polo and splashed around.

A bit before noon, Nurse Anne came in to tell us to get out and get ready for lunch. We got out, showered, got dressed, and started to make our way down toward lunch. Louis and I were stopped by Nurse Darcy when we tried to go into the dining hall. "The two of you are having lunch with a special visitor. Follow me."

She took us to a different part of the hospital that I had never seen before. It was much nicer than the other parts. Louis leaned over to me and explained, "This is the wing they show visitors, because they don't want to show them where the patients live."

Nurse Darcy guided us into a beautiful dining room. It was brightly painted in yellow and had an antique wood-stained table in the centre and a buffet cabinet on the side of the room. The table was set for three, with crystal glasses, blue Wedgewood plates and bowls, and newly polished silverware. Nurse Darcy told us to take a seat and left the room. Louis looked like he had seen a ghost. I guided him to a chair, poured him some water, and handed it to him. He gazed up at me and said two words, "Mr. Garrett."

I sat myself down, and I felt myself get faint. I looked to Louis, who seemed confused by my faintness.

Before Mr. Garrett had walked in, I explained to him how I knew the ferry man. "He brought me here."

Louis did not even have time to react. Mr. Garrett waltzed into the room and took a seat at the end of the table between Louis and I.

6
Back to the Beginning

A SHOUT FROM upstairs interrupted Luther's story. Elizabeth looked up from her cup of coffee with a worried look as Luther ran upstairs to see what was wrong, only to find Benjamin on the floor. He had fallen off the small chair Luther had put him on and was too weak to get up.

What was in the tea last night? Benjamin wondered.

Luther offered help to Benjamin, and the lawyer warily accepted. The ferry man helped Benjamin to get up and go down the stairs to where Elizabeth was sitting. Luther guided Benjamin to the chair beside Elizabeth and asked Benjamin if he would like some coffee. Benjamin nodded slowly. Luther stood at his kitchen counter, brewed some coffee, and took a seat again at the table while he waited.

Benjamin yelled in a fit of rage and asked a million questions. "What did you do to my father? Why do I feel weak? Why did you bring Elizabeth downstairs and not me? And why can't we leave?"

Luther slowly turned to him, and calmly replied, "Young man, you should not speak like that to one who took you in at a time of need." He tried to hide the grin on his face while he spoke.

Benjamin continued yelling, "You can't keep us here! We're leaving!" He went to storm out, but he was feeling faint because of hunger.

"Benjamin, why don't you sit with Elizabeth and me, and drink some coffee and eat something as you listen to my story? All will make sense soon. I did not tell you the first part of the story because you know it quite well, and you needed to rest. I know your father used to tell you the story of the missing family and the small boy who was sent to the hospital by the ferry man; you just never knew that the boy was me and that the ferry man was your grandfather."

Benjamin sat there in shock. Luther had dropped this bomb on him, and he did not know how to react. He was not sure if he should be sad or angry at his father, who had lied to him about his grandfather.

"Why should I believe you?" Benjamin finally asked.

"Because you know your grandfather's business was shady and full of lies."

Benjamin knew he couldn't argue with that. His father used to talk about not wanting to take over the family

41

business, but he would never fully explain why. He would always just say that his father had been up to no good.

"Benjamin, I am sure you might be very upset with your father for not telling you this, but why don't you sit and listen to the rest of my story. It will fill in the missing pieces of what your father told you," Luther explained to him.

"Now, where was I?" he continued. "Ah, yes, so your grandfather, Mr. Garrett, had just sat down between Andrew Harland and I inside the Rideau Regional Hospital."

. . .

Mr. Garrett was dressed head to toe in black—black dress shoes, black slacks, a black pullover sweater, a black cap, and a black trench coat over top. He looked as if he had just come from a funeral. He took off his coat and hung up his hat. I looked at him with sadness in my eyes and waited for him to speak. Mr. Garrett slowly lifted his head, for he had been fixated on his shoes before so as not to make eye contact. He knew how upset I was.

Finally, he spoke. "I am in love with a newly widowed woman, Helen, from Perth, the next town over, and she's expecting a baby. She told me she would leave me if I did not get you the help you need. You both were so delusional over what happened to your parents and siblings. Louis, you confronted me, saying I killed them, and Luther, you were so convinced that they had run away from you. You scared Helen. I had to bring you here to get you help."

Louis and I looked at each other, dumbfounded and unsure of what to say. Neither of us had ever heard of Helen. I went to speak up when I was again interrupted by Mr. Garrett, who said, "I must leave to attend Helen's husband's funeral."

And with that, he left the room through a different door than we had entered and slammed the door behind him. I could not help but wonder where that door led. I later learned that it was a different entrance to keep families from finding out what the hospital looked like.

My thoughts were interrupted by Nurse Darcy, who put her hand on my shoulder, as if to show affection for me in that tough time. "Pick up your lunches and follow me."

We followed her back down the hallway and into the games room. She got out two yellow TV trays from the stack in the corner of the room and set them up in front of the couch. She acted like she was trying to cheer us up.

Louis and I sat in silence as we ate our lunches. I was the first to speak.

"Why did he come visit?" I asked Louis. "He barely said anything."

"Maybe he just wanted to see if we were okay."

"Then why would he tell us we were going crazy?" I blurted out. "Were we crazy?"

Louis looked at me like I had sprouted antlers. "Mr. Garrett is the one who's crazy. He killed my parents, your parents, and probably this Helen woman's husband."

"How do you know that Mr. Garrett killed your parents?" I asked, not really wanting to know the answer.

"He was the last person to see them alive. The police questioned him about it too, but I heard rumours that he bought them off."

I looked at him with tears in my eyes. Maybe Mr. Garrett really *had* killed my parents. Maybe he even killed my brothers.

7

A Man with a Badge

THE NEXT MORNING, I woke up to Nurse Darcy coming into my room to give me my morning medication.

"Good morning, Luther," she greeted me. "Please take this."

She handed me a small blue cup. I looked down to see the arrangement of colours, shapes, and sizes in the cup.

"What are all of these?" I questioned.

"Mostly vitamins and a few pills to keep you happy."

"Does everyone get these?"

"Yes, they do."

I shrugged it off and downed it. I followed it with a drink of water.

"Thank you, Luther," she said as she headed out the door to continue her rounds.

Once she left the room, I grabbed my journal and propped the pillows up in my bed. A small yellow piece of paper fell out of my journal. I remembered that it was the note from Nurse Darcy. I opened it.

Dearest Luther,

Meet me in room 603 at midnight tomorrow night.

From,
Darcy

On the back of the note was a small map drawn of how to get to room 603. Just then, Nurse Anne walked into the room, so I shoved the note back into my journal and put the journal in my bedside drawer.

"Good morning, Luther. You have ten minutes until breakfast, so you better start getting ready," she said in a huffed voice as she hurried out of the room.

I could not help but think about the note in my journal. *What does Nurse Darcy want to talk to me about?*

I jumped out of bed, put on a new blue uniform that was folded neatly in my drawer, went down the hall to brush my teeth, and headed down the long corridor to breakfast. I sat at what was becoming my regular table with the boys. We sat there and talked about what games we would play that afternoon in the game room while we waited for breakfast to be served.

Breakfast was French toast, scrambled eggs, and orange slices with white milk. We all ate quickly since French toast was our favourite. After breakfast, I headed to the library and signed out a new book to read, and then went back to my room.

I lay on my bed and opened my book. I had gotten through fifteen pages before I was interrupted by a knock on the door.

Nurse Anne walked in and said, "Sit up. You have a visitor."

My heart fluttered. *Has Mr. Garrett come back for me? Can I forgive him for abandoning me here? What about what he might have done to my parents?* A million things were going through my head as I worked up the courage to face Mr. Garrett.

I was disappointed when a man walked in, dressed in black, with a black belt, a shiny silver badge, and a police hat.

"Good morning, Luther," he said to me. "Don't be worried. You didn't do anything. I just need to ask you a few questions about Mr. Garrett. I heard you lived with him for a while before he brought you here?"

I nodded in reply to his question. I was not worried to see the police officer there. I knew Mr. Garrett had already donated a bunch of money to them for the cops to stop asking questions.

He pulled out my desk chair, took a seat, brought out his small black notebook, and clicked his pen. He was ready to write.

"Who are your parents?"

I quickly answered. "Sarah and Thomas Neville."

The constable nodded and wrote something down. He continued with his next question: "Luther, do you know where your parents live now?"

I replied with a shake of my head as I told him what Mr. Garrett had said about my parents. "My parents ran away because they didn't want me." A tear ran down my face as I finished.

He looked at me with pity but tried to brush it off with a smile as he asked his next question. "Luther, can you tell me about Mr. Garrett? How did he treat you?"

"Mr. Garrett was like a father to me. I loved him, and he loved me. He always treated me well. He clothed me, fed me, entertained me, and took me in when nobody wanted me. He was a great man," I explained.

"Luther, do you think Mr. Garrett would hurt you?"

"No, I never felt unsafe in his presence. He made me feel safe and loved."

"Thank you, Luther. I will see you around." And with that, he walked out of my room and whispered something to Nurse Anne at the nurse's station.

Feeling uneasy about the police officer's visit, I spent the day in my room.

Later that day, during dinner, the boys told me they were all asked a million questions about Mr. Garrett and myself by the police officer.

"What kind of questions did they ask you?" I asked them.

"The police officers asked if I had ever felt in danger around you," Max explained.

"Oh yeah, he asked me that question too," Gabe piped in. "He also asked if I knew if you ever committed a crime you were not caught for."

I was so confused about why this police officer had asked them these questions.

"The man asked me how well I knew Mr. Garrett, and if he was a trustworthy person," Louis explained.

"Why do you think he was asking all these questions?" I asked the guys.

"Maybe he's finally getting caught," Louis answered.

"I hope so," Max concluded.

"Me too," Gabe agreed.

I just nodded. I never thought Mr. Garrett was capable of murder.

Little did we know, I was the one being caught for something I did not do.

8

A Forbidden Love Story

AFTER THAT EXCITING day of events, the guys and I spent the evening in the games room as we played cards and laughed at the crazy day of questions. We were interrupted just after ten by Nurse Anne telling us it was time to return to our rooms.

We cleaned up our cards and bid goodnight to each other. I walked back slowly to my room. I tried to waste time since I had to meet Nurse Darcy at midnight. Once in my room, I pulled my journal out of my desk drawer.

I climbed into bed and propped up my pillow. After opening my journal, I wrote the date on the top. I had now been in the Rideau Regional Hospital for two weeks. I had started to get used to it. The nurses were very nice, and I had been treated well. I had a new routine, but I still missed my old routine with Mr. Garrett. I thought about the stories I had heard about hospitals like this. I was confused that I felt so comfortable and so at home there.

Something felt off. I decided to write in my journal about where I had been in the hospital. I wondered if maybe I had missed something. Maybe there was another section where people did not get treated as well. I got so caught up with my entry that, when I looked up to the nurse's station clock that was right outside my door, it said 11:55.

I jumped up. I had five minutes to find where Nurse Darcy wanted to meet. I slipped my robe on over my pyjamas, put my journal underneath my pillow, and left my room.

I started down the long corridor with Nurse Darcy's hand-drawn map in my hand. At the very end of the main hallway, I saw the red door shown on Nurse Darcy's map. I slowly opened the door, trying not to make a sound, and headed up three flights of stairs to the third floor. I opened the third-floor staircase door and went to the fourth door on the right as Nurse Darcy had drawn in her map.

I opened the door, only to find another set of stairs. The stairs curled up to a small hole in the ceiling of the room. I climbed the stairs and found myself in a tiny, white room. The room had a little window in the corner, which had bars over it and a stool beside it, where Nurse Darcy was perched.

"Hello, Luther," she greeted me. "We're standing in the room where you'll be moved next week once the paperwork goes through. I need to tell you a story.

51

"The officer who was here today thinks that you murdered your parents and brothers, because Mr. Garrett tried to pin it on you. They're trying to get you to slip up as they ask you questions about Mr. Garrett. The other nurses are now concerned for their safety, so they tried to convince the head of the hospital to move you to a more secure room."

I looked at her and started to cry. "I would never kill my parents or my brothers," I said in between sobs.

She nodded. "I know you aren't capable of this, but I know that Mr. Garrett is." She continued, "Luther, I think I must tell you something. I know Mr. Garrett very well. I am his daughter."

. . .

Mr. Garrett married my mother, Lucy, when she was seventeen. Her parents sold her to my dad, who was quite a few years older than her, because her parents were very poor and could not take care of her anymore. They were married a few months after they met, needing to make it official. They moved in together immediately after the wedding. They fell in love. Or at least, she fell in love with him. She used to tell me stories of all the happy times they had together. They had me a year after they got married. We were a contented family.

The night after I turned fifteen, Mr. Garrett, my dad, had just tucked me into bed and went downstairs to drink tea with my mother. I was half asleep when I heard my mother scream. I tried to sit up to go see what was wrong, but I could not move. I lay there all night, worried about my mother. Finally, my dad came to wake me up, and I asked about Mother. He sat at the end of my bed and told me she'd left in the middle of the night, because she did not want to be part of our family anymore.

I cried for three days. I never came out of my room. Mr. Garrett brought up all my meals to my room. He seemed genuinely sad too. My dad and I eventually got into a good routine. Until one day when he was away at work at the ferry, and I was home reading. I had gotten bored and looked around the living room, only to see a floorboard peaking up.

I walked over to the floorboard to determine why it was not in line with the rest of the floor. I pushed on the floorboard to flatten it to the others' level, but something stopped it, so I pulled up the floorboard a bit to see what the problem was. It was my mother, decayed under the floorboards, covered in blood. I screamed at the top of my lungs, but nobody could hear me.

I ran up the grand staircase to my room, got out my carpet bag, and packed everything I could. I knew I had to get out of there. I did not want to end up dead or in jail. I knew how much my father donated to the police academy, so they would not touch him. I grabbed my overcoat and boots and ran out the door. I went down to the river and uncovered the old wooden rowboat my dad kept at the lakeside for fishing. I threw my bag into the small boat, pushed it into the lake, and climbed in. I dipped my oars into the water and rowed across the lake. I did not want to take the ferry, because I didn't want my dad to see me leave. Once I got to the opposite shore, I pulled the boat up and ran toward the road.

I was able to catch a ride into the next town over, Smiths Falls, with a nurse from the Rideau Regional Centre, who looked to be about thirty-five.

"Thank you for giving me a ride," I said as I climbed into her station wagon.

"You're welcome. Where are you headed?" the nurse asked.

I burst into tears. "I don't know."

"You don't know where your going?"

More tears rushed down my face. "I'm running away from home," I started. "I needed to leave. It was dangerous."

"Did you go to the police?" She looked at me with her face full of worry.

"I can't."

"Yes, you can. I am taking you to the police station."

"No!" I pleaded.

"They'll help you," she said, her voice raised.

"No, they won't. My father is Mr. Garrett, the man who runs the ferry!" I yelled between sobs.

"Oh." She paused for a moment, like she did not know what to say. "I've heard he's a man that you do not want to mess with. Is it true that he pays all kinds of money to the police and hospital so he can control them?"

"Yes, a scary police officer comes to our door every month, and Dad hands them a cheque," I softly said. "I never knew what he was doing until I started to hear the whispering around town and was able to put all the pieces together."

"You can come stay with me," she explained.

"I just met you. I don't even know your name."

"My name is Anne; I work at Rideau Regional Hospital. I have an apartment that is attached to the hospital, where I have a spare bedroom," Anne explained.

"Nice to meet you, Anne. My name is Darcy Garrett. How will I repay you?"

"Well, Darcy, you can come work underneath me at the hospital."

"But I'm not a nurse."

"You can study to become one at the hospital once you turn sixteen. There's a nursing school attached to our hospital, so between your studies, you can work with me."

"Wow, thank you so much, Anne."

We arrived at the hospital and drove down the long driveway lined with beautiful maple trees that had leaves that were changing colours to a dark orange. We pulled into the parking lot at the hospital, and I followed Anne into the building. We arrived at an office, and she knocked on the door.

"Come in," a man answered.

Anne turned the doorknob and pushed the door open, revealing a middle-aged man sitting behind a desk.

"Hello, Mr. Maison. This is my new friend, Darcy; she would like to be a nurse when she grows up."

"Hi, Darcy. That is great to hear. I am Mr. Maison, and I'm in charge of the nursing school here at the Rideau Regional Centre. How old are you?"

"I'm fifteen."

"Great, so you can watch and learn with Anne until you turn sixteen, and then you can start your studies and start to work on your own," Mr. Maison explained.

"Thank you, sir."

"Nurse Anne, why don't you take Darcy with you over to the nurses' quarters and get a room set up for her," Mr. Maison said.

"Will do. She can stay in the spare bedroom in my apartment here on the hospital campus," Anne explained.

We left Mr. Maison's office, and I followed Nurse Anne down the stairs to the basement and down the long corridor to a black door, which led us through a tunnel to a different building. I later learned it was the nurse's apartment building.

She unlocked the door to what must have been her apartment, went to her linen closet, and pulled out a pair of sheets, a few blankets, and a pillow.

"Welcome to your new home," Anne said as she walked to her linen closet. "Here, help me set up the couch for you tonight, and then tomorrow, when I am showing you around the hospital, the maintenance men can come in and set up your room."

I lay on her couch that night and wondered what my dad had thought when he arrived home and I was not there. At some point, I must have drifted off to sleep, because I woke up to Anne calling my name.

"Darcy? Darcy, it is time to wake up."

I opened my eyes to find Anne staring down at me, holding a pile of freshly pressed clothes.

"Here, put these on." She handed me a newly pressed red and white striped dress with a white apron, white undergarments, white socks, and white canvas shoes. "Go ahead and shower; then we can start my rounds."

I nodded and quickly did what I was told. Before long, we were walking through the tunnel toward the hospital.

I followed Nurse Anne around as she visited all the patients, giving medications and checking vitals. I watched and learned as Nurse Anne helped patients with their day. Around seven, Nurse Anne told me that our shift was over and that we could return to her living corridors. We went down the stairs to the basement, through the tunnel, and through the black door at the end of the hallway.

We walked into Nurse Anne's apartment to find a few maintenance workers had converted Nurse Anne's office space into a bedroom for me.

"Hi, you must be Darcy," one of the maintenance men said.

"Yeah, I am. Thank you for bringing furniture up for me."

"No problem. We have some things left over from a young lady who moved out a few months ago, so we put it in your room, so it would feel like home," the second maintenance man said.

"Thank you."

"You're welcome. Have a good night, ladies."

Anne and I waved goodbye to the men as we shut the door behind them. I walked toward my new room. The room was painted dusty pink, and they had set up a small bed in the corner with a light pink bedspread. Next to my bed was a little nightstand with a lamp on it, and across the room was a plain white desk. I heard a soft knock on my door, and I turned to see Nurse Anne in the doorway.

She held a large canvas bag and said to me, "Hello, I've brought you a few things that one of the nurses gave to me when I first came here. I thought you might like some of it."

"Thank you!" I exclaimed as I put the bag on my bed.

"Did you enjoy following me around today?"

"Yeah, I think this is the perfect job for me. I love helping people," I explained.

"Well, we both had a long day today, so I am going to go get some sleep. Goodnight, Darcy."

"Goodnight, Anne. Thank you again. For everything."

I shut my door behind her, walked over to the bag, and dumped its contents onto my bed. Out of the bag came a bunch of nursing textbooks, a little brown stuffed bear with a red heart sewn in the middle of its stomach, some fun pens, and a key ring with four skeleton keys on it.

I examined the keys, and I found that each had a small inscription on it: 603; 807; 928; and 763. I could not help but wonder what they unlocked. I put my white sweater on over my white and red striped dress, put the keys in the small pocket on the dress, slipped on my white canvas shoes, and headed out into the living room.

"Hey, Anne, would be okay if I went for a walk to explore the building?"

"Sure, just be careful, alright?"

"I will, and Anne, I found a few keys in the canvas bag you gave me. What are they for?"

"I think they're just to get around to different buildings. They were in the bag when I got it from the last nurse."

"Oh, okay. They each have numbers on them. Do you think that corresponds to rooms?"

"It might. What are the numbers?"

"Numbers 603, 807, 928, and 763."

"Those are old patient rooms in the basement. Most of them anyway. You can go check them out if you want. They aren't being used right now."

"Okay, thank you," I said as I walked out the door.

I headed back through the tunnel, through the black door, and into the basement of the hospital.

I looked down at the keys again, checking the numbers. I knew I couldn't ask for help to find these rooms, so I started down the long hallway in the basement, checking every room number and peering down every corridor.

I finally found room 763, slipped the old key into the lock, and slowly turned it, having to wiggle the key to unlock it fully. I turned the doorknob, saying a little prayer, and opened the door. I peered inside the dark room and felt around for a light. My hand landed on a chain, which I pulled, and the room filled with light.

I looked around the room, but a wall of photographs caught my eye. There had to be a dozen photos of families pinned with red tacks onto the yellowed wall. All the families looked so happy. They smiled, with their kids in front, dressed in their best. I wondered what they all had in common, and why their photos were all pinned onto this wall. I continued to look around the room to see if there was a connection to all these photos when my eyes landed on an old brown filing cabinet.

I walked toward it and pulled the first drawer. It was stuck, so I pulled as hard as I could. The drawer came loose, and I flew back and hit the wall with a loud *umph!* I hoped no one had heard me hit the wall as I stood up, brushed off the dust on my dress, and removed the first file from the draw. It was labelled "Harland." I opened the file, and a picture of a boy dropped to the floor. I picked it up and turned the photo over. It read:

Louis Harland
Patient #4536
Parents: Murdered

I put the photo back into the file and picked up the next. Again, inside the file was a small photo and the back of it read.

Max Delbert
Patient #6577
Parents: Murdered

I started to see a pattern and quickly picked up another file.

Silas Axton
Patient #3245
Parents: Murdered

And another one:

Andrew Hadley
Patient #5567
Parents: Murdered

I picked up the next file to see if the patterned continued.

Gabe Thurmond
Patient #8698
Parents: Murdered

I knew the next file would be the same, but I checked anyway.

Jack Garrett
Patient #6034
Mother: In danger

I looked closer at the last photo I held. Jack Garrett . . . curious that he shared a last name with me. I sat on the floor and opened the file. It read:

Name: Jack Garrett
Patient #6034
Reason for admission: Father, Jack Garrett, and mother, Lucy Garrett, bought Jack Garrett in when he was six months old. Jack Garrett Senior said Jack Garrett Junior would not stop screaming during the night.
Nurse's notes:
Six-month check-in: Jack Garrett is a very well-behaved child.
1-year check-in: Behaving well, developing on track.
2-year check-in: A very happy two-year-old.
5-year check-in: In a routine, doing well.
10-year check-in: Moved to secured room.
Missing

I almost dropped the file, because it then hit me that this boy was my brother.

9

The Lost Boy

NURSE DARCY LOOKED up at me with sadness in her eyes. She had gone pale and stopped telling her story. I walked over closer to her in the small white room and gave her a long, warm hug as a tear ran down her face.

"Where is your brother now?"

She looked up at me with a blank stare and said one word: "Dead."

A dizzy feeling came upon me as I slid down the wall, and I took a seat on the ground. It was hard to think as I looked around the room that the doctors wanted to move me into.

I could not help but think, *Will I die here too?*

Nurse Darcy saw panic in my eyes. She assured me that she was doing everything she could to save me from being put up here.

. . .

Benjamin interrupted Luther's story by clearing his throat. "Luther, Jack Garrett Junior is my father, and he isn't dead, or at least, he wasn't until last night . . ." His voice trailed off as he thought about the previous night's events.

"Benjamin, let me finish the story; it will all make sense soon," Luther replied.

"No," Benjamin said.

"No?" Luther asked.

"I am sure he didn't mean *no*," Elizabeth jumped in, frightened of what Luther might do to Benjamin.

"You don't need to speak for me, Elizabeth," Benjamin snarled.

Elizabeth looked at Benjamin with her eyes full of hurt. She knew they didn't know each other, but she had thought they were in this together.

Benjamin saw the hurt in Elizabeth's eyes, and he started to soften.

Luther interrupted the moment. "I am sure Benjamin did not mean that, Elizabeth."

"Leave her alone, Luther. Don't try to get her on your side right now. This is between you and me," Benjamin huffed

"Calm down, Benjamin," Elizabeth tried to tell him.

"No, I can't calm down! This man has kidnapped us, is holding us against our will, and killed my father!" Benjamin yelled.

"You are more than welcome to leave, Benjamin." Luther paused for a moment. "But then you won't ever know what happened to your father or why."

Benjamin knew Luther was right. If he did not stay, he would never find out what happened to his father.

"Elizabeth doesn't need to stay; you can let her go," Benjamin continued.

"See, that is where you're wrong. Elizabeth's family is as much a part of this story as yours."

Elizabeth, who had been trying to stay out of the argument, finally finished it by saying, "Benjamin, let's just sit here for a little longer and listen to the story."

"Fine."

"Alright, where was I?" Luther said as he continued his story. "Oh, yes, the part about the letters." As Luther restarts his story, he pulls out a large folder and sets it on the table.

. . .

Nurse Darcy checked her watch. One in the morning. She looked at me with a sad expression and told me I had to get back to my room before the one-thirty check. She gave me a hug, lingered for a moment with me in her arms, and then bid me goodnight. She made me feel like I was going to be okay. I knew she would keep me safe. I made my way back down the curly set of stairs, along the hall, and slowly headed back to what seemed like an amazing room to be in after seeing where they wanted to move me. As soon as I entered my room, I took out my journal and wrote down all my friends' names. I knew I needed to talk to them tomorrow to find out what they knew. I slid my journal under my pillow and drifted off to sleep.

Morning came early. Nurse Anne awakened me just after six and told me it was time for my shower and bed change. I slowly pulled myself out of bed, and a male nurse came into the room to take me for a shower. We walked down the hall together and made some small talk. We entered the shower room and headed toward a stall. The male nurse, whose name I had learned was Paul, handed me a towel, a face cloth, shampoo, and a bar of soap. I thanked him as he walked toward the door. I jumped into the cold shower and quickly washed.

I dried myself off and met with Nurse Paul again as I headed out the door. He gave me a nod and a small smile as I went back to my room. I dressed in a pair of new blue uniform pants and top. I slipped on my white socks and pulled on my white canvas shoes. I brushed my hair and teeth and headed down the long corridor for breakfast. I sat down at my regular table with my friends, but none of them were there yet. I looked at the big yellow clock on the wall, which read 6:45. I was early. Just after seven, my friends came flooding into the dining hall.

They sat down next to me with blank expressions on their faces. I leaned over to Louis and asked what was wrong, but he just shrugged it off. None of the boys would look me in the eye. They all sat in silence and looked at their plates of eggs, toast, home fries, and bacon. We ate in silence, which was very unusual for our table of friends, but I shrugged it off as everyone maybe being tired. I tried not to worry and thought about Nurse Darcy, which made me a bit happier. She had been in my thoughts since we'd met the previous night in room 603. I should've felt scared and worried after our conversation, but instead I just couldn't stop thinking of her.

Breakfast was eaten, and then we were excused back to our rooms. Louis slipped me a small folded white note as we walked out. I ran to my room to open it.

Meet up at 10 p.m. Be there.

I refolded the note and shoved it into my pocket just as Nurse Darcy came in.

She looked at me and asked, "What did you just put in your pocket?"

I sheepishly pulled out the note from Louis and handed it to her. She read it, then gave it back to me as she looked me in the eye.

"I will see you there," she quietly told me.

Before I could ask why and what was going on, she left the room.

Time went by slower than pouring molasses in the middle of winter. At lunch and dinner, nobody talked at our table. We all listened to the busy hum of the other children and nurses in the dining hall. We got strange looks from the nurses, who knew us as chatterboxes.

It had felt like the longest day of my life when Nurse Anne came in and told me it was time for bed.

"Lights out," she said and left as quickly as she had come.

I crawled under my blankets and laid awake, watching the clock as it ticked away, hoping that ten would come around quicker.

9:30

9:31

9:32

9:33

I watched the small hand go around the clock for every second that it ticked, and it seemed as if my heart beat faster as well.

9:42

9:43

9:44

9:45

So close, only fifteen more minutes.

9:46

9:47

9:48

9:49

9:50

I slowly got up and started to make my way to our basement hangout room. I turned down the long corridor and toward a rarely used staircase that the boys had found out about. I pulled a little red knob in the middle of the wall, and it greeted me with a small dark opening. I crouched and used my arms to pull my body through.

Once I was inside the wall, I looked around the tiny room for the hatch in the corner. I walked over to the hatch and pulled it open with a hard tug, revealing a creaky wooden staircase. I gingerly stepped down the stairs to expose another red door. I knew that door well as it was the door to our hangout room. I opened it to reveal Louis, Max, Silas, Andrew, Gabe, and Nurse Darcy.

"Hello, Luther." Louis was the first to talk as he waved to me.

I nodded in acknowledgement.

Louis started to say something, but Nurse Darcy interrupted him, almost as if she could not hold it in any longer.

"You're in danger!" she broke down with a shout. "I am so sorry, Luther." Nurse Darcy looked as if she was about to reach out for me but forced herself not to.

I looked to her, wishing I could just give her a hug, rub her back, and tell her it would be okay. I wanted to stop her worrying. My thoughts were interrupted by Louis, who continued the obviously rehearsed intervention. Each had a part to say and a time to say it.

"We think you should run away, Luther," Louis said as he looked at his shoes. "You need to leave town and get far away from here and Mr. Garrett."

I looked at all of them standing there like they were crazy. They looked back at me with so much love and friendship in their eyes, as they were all worried for my life.

I thought, *I know they're right*. I thought harder. *I know they're right, but I don't want to leave these amazing friends I've made. And I don't want to leave Nurse Darcy.*

I looked around the room to see if anyone else had anything to say, but everyone stayed quiet. I finally spoke up. "I don't need to leave."

"Yes, you do," Max argued back.

"No, I'm not meant to be in this hospital, so I need to find out why I was put here. There must be an answer."

"You aren't safe here," Darcy pleaded.

"I can't leave!" I yelled.

Everyone's heads shot up to look at me.

I paced the room. "Nurse Darcy found folders with all of our names, and each folder had one thing in common: Our parents were murdered. Someone needs to solve this mystery. Every single resident who lives in this centre and has a file like that deserves to see the truth and learn how their parents died. There is a killer on the loose, and I am going to catch him."

The boys looked surprised by the news they had just received.

Nurse Darcy fell to her knees and started to cry. She softly whispered, "Jack," thinking of her brother, so softly that I was the only one who heard.

Silas was the first to talk. He quietly said, "I want to know how this was allowed to happen, and how we all got stuck here."

I looked at him with surprise in my eyes.

Gabe stepped up next to speak. "I have an old file that the police gave me when my parents went missing; it might help."

"Where is it?" I asked him.

"It's in my room," Gabe answered.

"How did you sneak it into the hospital?" Max questioned.

"I hid it in my coat when I was brought into the hospital, and then I stashed it under my mattress," Gabe explained.

"Okay, that could be helpful," I said. "Who else is in?"

Andrew looked to me with sadness in his eyes and said, "I'm in."

Max nodded along in agreement.

Nurse Darcy spoke up next. "Here's the key for the room with all the old files. We should check it out tomorrow night." She held up the key, showing myself and the boys.

Louis joined in as he moved toward us and helped create the plan, "We can all meet here again tomorrow night at ten. We'll go with Darcy and check out the files, and Max, bring yours as well."

We all murmured our agreement.

"I'll bring my notebook so we can keep track of it all, and as soon as we put together a list of suspects, we can go to the police," I told them.

"No!" they all shouted in unison.

"No police," Silas continued. "They're not on our side."

"Why?" I asked.

"We've all had to deal with the police after our parents' deaths, and all of us were accused of their murders. Not even a single suspect was detained. They are not on our side," Silas explained.

"Fine, once we can prove who the killer is, we'll find a way to deal with them ourselves," I replied.

"How are we going to do that?" Gabe questioned.

"I don't know . . ." I said, my voice trailing off. I hadn't thought that far through the plan. "All I know is we need to catch them and make sure they don't kill anyone else."

Nurse Darcy looked like she was going to be sick. Louis noticed and suggested we all go back to our rooms and finish the plan when we met up the next day.

We all agreed and returned to our rooms. Each of us left five minutes apart so that we did not get caught together.

I watched as Nurse Darcy headed down the basement hallway and toward the tunnel to her apartment. At that time, I did not realize how much I was in love with her.

When it was my turn to go, I headed back up the stairs, snuck past the night-shift officers, and slipped into my room.

I climbed into my nicely made bed and slowly drifted off into a deep sleep.

. . .

I was rudely awoken by two strong hands grabbing either arm and lifting me out of bed. I tried to open my eyes, but I couldn't see anything. It was then that I felt that something was covering my eyes. I felt another pair of strong hands as two people carried me out of the room, and what I assumed, was down the hall.

I was dropped onto a soft bed, and then I was being strapped in. I struggled with the people strapping me in, but they were much stronger than me. I was rolled down the corridor, the wheels on the bed clicking as we went. A loud beep sounded as we went over a bump, and then there was the sound of a large metal door slamming behind us.

I wanted to scream, but I doubted anyone would hear me. I had the sensation of raising up and assumed we had rolled into a large freight elevator. After it stilled, and we travelled down several more corridors, we must have gotten to our destination since I felt the tight straps being lifted off and the cold, strong hands wrap around my arms once again. Someone took the blindfold off, tossed me into a small white room, and slammed the door behind me. I fell to my knees from the powerful throw, then lifted my head and looked around the room.

Nurse Darcy was right. I was in the room she'd brought me to earlier.

I heard the door open again, and I quickly turned to see who it was. I looked up to see a very tall man in perfectly pressed white scrubs and a nurse whom I hadn't met.

"Where am I?" I yelled.

He did not answer.

"Why am I here?"

Nothing.

"I want out!" I yelled, running toward the door.

He didn't say anything as he grabbed me, picked me up, then lay me on the small ratty bed in the corner as I screamed and struggled to move. His grip grew tighter as he held me down so the nurse could insert a needle into my arm.

Suddenly, I felt drowsy, frozen, and sick.

The next thing I knew, the room went black.

10
Day Seven

I WOKE UP in a panicked sweat, not knowing what day it was. I lay on the cold floor, surrounded by blood. I heard the door open, but I was too weak to turn around to see who it was. I slowly raised my head, hoping it was someone who was going to save me. To my surprise, it was Nurse Darcy.

"Hi, Luther." A relieved but worried look came across her face as she knelt to help me stand up.

"Hi," was all I could get out. I felt too weak to talk.

She got me on my feet, and I put my arm around her shoulder as she helped me to the bed. She pulled a cookie and a bottle of pop out of her red and white candy-striped dress.

"Here, eat this. It will give you some energy," she said as she handed me the cookie; then she opened the pop and put it on the nightstand next to me.

"Thank you." I gladly accepted it, as I could not remember when I had eaten last.

I finished the cookie and juice as Nurse Darcy helped me lay down on the bed. My eyes were heavy as I tried to fight the sleep.

"Get some sleep, Luther," Darcy said. "I'll try to be here when you wake up."

I stopped fighting and instantly fall asleep.

When I woke up, I saw Nurse Darcy at the end of my bed. I tried to sit up, but as soon as I did, pain shot through my stomach. I lifted my blue shirt and looked down to see a large cut across my stomach, which appeared to be stitched up in an ivory zigzag line. I looked up to Nurse Darcy, who had pity in her eyes. She kissed her two fingers and then very gently grazed those fingers along the wound.

"What happened to me?" I asked, looking at my new scar.

"You don't remember? They had to perform emergency surgery; your appendix was about to burst." She pulled a small orange bottle out of her red and white striped dress.

"Put out your hand," she told me as she undid the cap.

I did as I was told, and two long white pills fell into my hand.

"What are these for?" I asked.

"They will help the pain," she explained to me as she handed me a cup of water.

"Okay." I had always trusted Nurse Darcy; she had never given me a reason not to, so I put the pills in my mouth and washed them down with a full cup of water. Setting the cup on my nightstand, I struggled to sit up from the pain and weakness as Darcy moved toward me to help.

"Has anything happened this week since you've been in this room?"

A week? I've been here a week? She must be wrong. I'm supposed to meet up with her and the boys tonight. It has not been a week.

She looked at me with fright, as I must have spoken my thoughts out loud, and took a calendar out of the blue bag she had sitting at her feet. She opened it up to September and pointed to the fourteenth.

"You don't remember this week at all?" she asked, with her eyes full of concern.

"No, I thought I had only been in here a day," I told her honestly.

"You have been here a week." Darcy looked frightened. "It's scary you don't remember a whole week."

I looked to the ground, not knowing how to reply. "Does that mean I missed the meet with the boys to discuss the killer?" I hoped that maybe they postponed it.

She shook her head no in response but pulled a large beige file folder out from her bag. She handed me the rather heavy file and said, "This is everything that we've compiled so far. The quicker we get this man, the quicker you get out of here. We want you to look at the file and put in some of

77

your own thoughts." She took out a red pen and handed it to me. "I'll be back to get it from you tomorrow. Don't let anyone see it."

"How did you get it in here?" I asked. "Isn't this wing full of security?"

"I changed with one of the newer nurses to be your nurse for the next few days, and I slipped the hall monitor a pack of cigarettes so he wouldn't say anything about the switch or the bag," Darcy explained. With that, she pulled herself off the bed and headed out the door.

11
The Folder

I HELD THE closed folder in my left hand and the red pen in my right. Something on the front of the folder caught my eye, and I pulled the folder closer to take a better look. Small blue letters on the bottom right corner said:

We will get you out of there soon.
- the boys

I smiled to myself as I thought about how much my friends cared about me. I sat up straighter on my small bed, moved the pillow to the wall, and pulled myself toward it to sit. I opened the folder and drew out the first paper. It looked like a medical report cover page. It had a patient number on it, a date, and a doctor's name, along with his signature. It was signed "Dr. Scott Wyatt."

Office of Chief Medical Examiner

City of Ottawa

Name of Decedent:	M.E. #:
Charlotte Axton	Q-24-078465

Autopsy Performed by:	Date of Autopsy:
Scott Wyatt, MD	05/28/1949

FINAL DIAGNOSES:

1. Strangling.
   A. Bruising of the neck.
   B. Fractures of the thyroid.
2. Abrasions of the left forearm.
3. Abrasions of the left torso, with:
   A. Abrasions, contusions, and
      subcutanous hemorrhages.
4. See toxicology report.
5. See neuropathology report.

Office of Chief Medical Examiner

City of Ottawa

Name of Decedent:	M.E. #:
Mateo Axton	Q-25-078466

Autopsy Performed by:	Date of Autopsy:
Scott Wyatt, MD	05/28/1949

FINAL DIAGNOSES:

1. Blunt Force Trauma to the head.
   A. Multiple lacerations, abrasions, and contusions of the skull including two large, branched, full thickness lacerations of the bilateral parietal scalp.
2. Abrasions of the left torso, with:
   A. Abrasions, contusions, and subcutanous hemorrhages.
3. Abrasion of the right cheek.
4. Abrasion/contusion posterior right shoulder
5. See toxicology report.
6. See neuropathology report.

I turned the page over, revealing an autopsy report for Charlotte and Mateo Axton, Silas' parents.

> *The remains of Mr. Mateo and Mrs. Charlotte Axton were discovered floating in a boat that had washed up onto shore. Both bodies were in an advanced state of decomposition due to exposure. I estimate time of death to have been 7 days previous. Cause of death for both is blunt force trauma to the skull.*

After I read the report, I had started to rethink what we were getting ourselves into. We were only just kids, being treated like criminals, locked up in this mental institution, and we were about to try to stop a killer. I reminisced about my old life when I was sheltered and did not know about the bad things going on in the world or the inter-workings of the mental hospital. I remembered that I was doing this to save my life and many others. I flipped to the next page.

It revealed a long-handwritten note written on old scraps of nurses' paper, which had started to turn yellow. I licked my thumb and ran it along the name on the top right-hand corner of the page. The ink smudged, which told me it had not been there long. The name on the top of the page read "Silas Axton." It appeared that Silas had written me a letter to help the investigation.

Dear Luther,

I hope you are doing well. It's not the same on the wing without you. I am writing this letter to tell you everything I know about Mr. Garrett and my parents' murder, and attached is the file from the police.

My parents and I were on our way back from visiting my aunt in Perth, and since Perth was on the opposite side of the water from our house, we were made to take the ferry home. Unfortunately, we left Perth too late in the day. We did not make it to the ferry before seven o'clock and were forced to stay at Mr. Garrett the ferryman's house.

My family was middle class. My father was always dressed in a tailored suit that my mother made for him. My mother always looked put together. Even when I had to identify her body, she was still wearing her favourite shade of red lipstick. She made all her dresses by hand and would always wear her curly hair up in a tight bun, with red lipstick perfectly applied on her lips to top off her look.

My father ran the local paper, and he had done many stories about the disappearance of people in our small town. You could tell he was on edge from the moment he walked through Mr. Garrett's door. But I knew he had always been curious about the inner works of Mr. Garrett's home.

Mr. Garrett led us into his living room and told us to make ourselves comfortable while he went and made some tea. The living room was nicely set up. It had long oak floorboards covering the floor, the walls were painted a warm yellow, and a bleach-white couch sat in the middle of the room accompanied by a matching white chair and a dark-red-stained coffee table. Paintings and old antique clocks covered the walls, and each one looked as different as the next. As soon as he left the room, my father pulled out his camera and started to capture Mr. Garrett's living room. He said to my mother, "No one has ever gotten the inside scoop from Mr. Garrett, and this kind of story will have the papers flying off the stand."

After he clicked the camera again, Mr. Garrett came flying into the room from the kitchen. He yelled at my father, asking him what he thought he was doing. My father pointed his camera and took one more picture of a weird-looking red and white picture in an old, light wood frame. The picture had a white background and was full of red spatters across the canvas.

That was Mr. Garrett's last straw. His face turned red, and he threw the pot of hot tea at my father, hitting him in the head. Bright red blood splattered onto the bleach-white couch, knocking him unconscious. I closed my eyes as soon as I saw the blood, and then I heard my mother scream. I opened my eyes to see Mr.

Garrett's hands on my mother's shoulders as blood and tears ran down her face. She looked directly at me and mouthed the word, "Run."

I paused for a second, knowing I would be leaving my mother behind to fight for herself, but I knew if I could make it out alive, I would be able to get Mr. Garrett arrested. I turned toward the door we had come in and ran as fast as I could in the direction of the water. The only way across was to swim. It was early June, so the water temperature was not bad when I jumped in, but my clothes were weighing me down as I swam. I kicked off my shoes and continued to work to the other side, knowing the full distance was a little under a mile. My family would always swim directly across each summer as a fun activity, so I knew I could make it. When I got to the other side, I could barely breathe. I coughed up some water but kept moving. I ran another four blocks, making it to my father's office.

One of his reporters was still in the bullpen, so I banged on the glass until he let me in. I was soaked and had some blood spatter on me, so he gave me a funny look. I told him to get to his typewriter and to type out the story I was about to tell him. It needed to go to print that evening. He sat down and I started telling him the story of my parent's murder. I wanted to think positive, to believe that my mom could still be alive, but I knew the stories of Mr. Garrett—he left no loose strings. The reporter started to type. He knew not to ask any questions or suggest calling the police. He covered the disappearances around town, and he was the one who had broken the story of the dirty cops in town.

The story was on the front page of the paper the following day. Less than 12 hours after my parents were murdered, I was arrested for their deaths. The police thought I did it. I tried to explain to the police that it was Mr. Garrett who killed them, and they explained to me that they had already talked to Mr. Garrett. He'd told them he'd witnessed me kill my parents.

I had to appear in court the following day, and I was represented by Luke Thurmond, whom I later found out was Gabe's dad. I was charged with both of my parents' murders, and their evidence against me was the blood spatter on my shirt and Mr. Garrett's witness testimony. The judge said that he could not trust a child's word over an adult's. He found me guilty and sentenced me to two years in the locked psych ward at Rideau Regional Hospital.

For four years, they ran every test in the book on me. For four years, I had to sit there for something I did not do while the real killer was walking around free and continued causing others harm. For four years, I was treated like a criminal. The nurses feared me. They would move to the other side of the room when they saw me walking down the hall.

People need to know that I did not kill my parents. Mr. Garrett finally needs to be caught and punished for what he did. I believe in you; I know you can figure out a way to solve this problem.

I hope to see you soon.

Sincerely,
Silas Axton

. . .

Luther wiped a tear from his eye before he returned the letter to the folder.

"Mr. Garrett killed these people just because they were taking photos of the inside of his home?" Elizabeth questioned.

"He did not like people who were nosy," Luther explained.

"I can't believe my grandfather would do something like this," Benjamin said in disbelief.

"He was a very bad man," Luther told Benjamin.

"Would your father talk about your grandfather when you were growing up, Benjamin?" Elizabeth asked.

"No." Benjamin paused. "My father never spoke of him, and when I did ask, he'd get a sad look on his face."

"I'm sorry, Benjamin," Elizabeth said as she placed her hand on Benjamin's, giving him a reassuring look.

"I need to continue the story; Benjamin, you need to hear the type of man your grandfather was," Luther said sternly as he pulled another letter out of his folder.

Benjamin nodded. He wanted to know more.

12
The Cult

I WIPED A tear from my eye after I read Silas' letter. I knew he had faith in me, which I needed. It helped me flip to the next page in the folder.

It was a clipped piece of a newspaper article. The header read, "Children Born in Newly Discovered Cult Sent to Rideau Hospital." Below the title was a picture of several children lined up in white clothing in front of the hospital. Each child had the same haircut and each had a straight-faced expression. Underneath the picture was a list of names, it named the children from left to right, and one was highlighted: Max Delbert.

Beneath the grouping of names was a ripped piece of the article, which read:

Police have received information regarding a cult that has operated secretly for the last fifteen years. Local police had suspicions that this cult existed but never had enough evidence to be certain until Mr. Garrett, a citizen of Rideau Ferry, discovered new information when he was approached to join the cult. Many cult members have since been found dead. Their children have been taken into the Rideau Regional Hospital's custody and will spend time in the psychiatric ward until they are deprogrammed from the cult.

The rest of the article had been torn off but attached to the article was another letter. This time it was from Max.

Luther,

I was told that writing this letter might help you solve the case.

My parents, Aaron and Scarlet Delbert, joined the Rideau cult at the age of twenty, and by the age of twenty-two, they had me. The Rideau cult was what the papers called a "friendship cult"—people would join for family and friendship. The preacher would reach out to lonely adults whose trust funds were their best friends. He would convince these people to live a better lifestyle, one full of healthy food, exercise, and relaxation by use of drugs; the preacher showed how much he cared for his followers—he treated them like family. The cult wanted its members to have many children to make the population of the cult grow, but after having me, my mom got very sick and was unable to have more children.

The cult did not live all together, so they wouldn't raise suspicions. Instead, the cult gave everyone a small piece of property on the Rideau, and a small wooden rowboat, which the members could use to get to the secluded island where the meetings were held. The cult would meet twice a week, once on Thursdays and once on Sundays. The island had a large grey barn in the centre, about a ten-minute walk from the docks. The inside of the barn was laid out like a mansion. It had white couches, matching chairs, and white-painted coffee tables. It had a big, completely white kitchen—even the dishes were white. The next room was a large white conference room. I often said the place looked like how I would imagine heaven. Upstairs was a small hospital room, for any members who were sick or giving birth, as well as a series of bedrooms and offices for reasons I never understood.

When the cult met, they would give sermons on the ideas of right and wrong, and how we should act in our everyday lives. Then we would all share a meal after the sermons. For most people, the cult was just a sense of family, people to eat meals with and share about your days, but most members did not know about the inner workings of upstairs. The rumours of upstairs were enough to give you nightmares—many people told tales of murder, prostitution, and theft. Members tried to keep

91

their children away from it all, but we still overheard the stories.

One afternoon, my family was sent out to get bread for the dinner gathering that the leaders of the cult were having. My mother offered to bake the bread, but she was instructed to get it from a small local bakery in Perth. The preacher told her they needed this special bread, and it would be ready at 6 p.m. I still wonder what the preacher had planned for the evening that included this "special bread." When we got to the bakery, they didn't have the bread ready yet, so we were forced to wait, which made us late for the ferry, and you know that the ferry man wouldn't run after 7 p.m., so we were stuck staying the night with Mr. Garrett. I could tell that Mr. Garrett was pleased with the idea of us having to stay with him. He had a grin on his face as he guided us toward his home. My parents knew he was suspicious of the cult because of the extra water traffic he had noticed lately. He was always on the water, so he knew everything about everyone's boat and the traffic on the water.

Mr. Garrett told me to make myself at home in his living room and then asked my parents to follow him downstairs, claiming that he needed their help. My parents followed Mr. Garrett down a set of stairs behind a creaky red door. As soon as I heard them reach the bottom step, I stood up and went after them. I heard my mother yell just as I opened the red door.

I silently made my way halfway down the steps so that I could see what was happening in the basement, but where they could not see me. I saw my father tied to a chair with blood running down his face, and my mother sitting on the floor, tied up and being forced to watch. I heard Mr. Garrett ask my parents a series of questions: "Where is the cult located? Who is Mason Sawyer? Where is the book?" My parents stayed very quiet and every five minutes, Mr. Garrett would hit my father again and ask the same three questions. Once Mr. Garrett had hit my father enough times that he was unresponsive and could no longer answer the questions, Mr. Garrett picked my mother off the floor.

He kept her hands tied but undid her feet so she could walk, and he started for the stairs. I ran from the stairs back into the living room and sat on the couch, pretending to look busy. I knew if I ran to the police, they would try to arrest my parents because Mr. Garrett would tell them about the cult. Mr. Garrett and my mother came into the room, and he told me to stand up and come with him. He led us to his rowboat, which was pulled up on shore, and instructed us to get in. He retied my mother's feet, pushed off the boat, and we started down the Rideau. He told my mother that, if she wanted to live, she would tell him how to get to the island the cult was on. My mother obeyed. She directed Mr. Garrett to the island.

We were about twenty feet away from the island when Mr. Garrett pushed my mother into the water.

Both her hands and feet were tied so she could not swim. I looked to the island to see if anyone was around for help, but it was silent. Now I know that everyone was in the pavilion. I tried to jump in after her, but Mr. Garrett pulled me back in. I had to watch my mother drown as he dragged me out of the boat onto shore, then headed toward the barn. I thought he would kill me next, but he never hurt me.

We took the path and walked ten minutes until we hit the barn, and Mr. Garrett instructed me to stay downstairs and not go anywhere. He left abruptly and ran upstairs. He was there for five minutes before members of the cult started entering the barn. Mr. Garrett had made Manson Sawyer, whom I later learned was the cult leader, call a mandatory meeting. Each family had been given a radio to have playing 24/7 in their homes; the preacher would broadcast from the island, using the radio for announcements and extra preaching times other than meetings.

Once everyone in the cult was accounted for, except my parents, Mr. Garrett exited the barn, only to return 20 minutes later with the sheriff and his detectives. I have no idea how they got there so fast. Mr. Garrett must have called the police when we left his house.

They arrested every adult in the barn and kept all the children in a big group. I counted about thirty-five kids. The children were first taken off the island on the police boat and then put onto a bus. The bus took us to Smiths

Falls and down a long lane, which we later found out was the Rideau Regional Hospital. We were unloaded and one by one checked into the hospital's psych ward. We were all put in a locked wing to be deprogrammed from the cult and were forbidden to talk to one another, not that we obeyed that rule. I heard one of the kids say one time that the adults had been taken to Kingston Penitentiary for all the various crimes that the cult had committed, and Mr. Garrett was called a hero for taking down the cult.

I don't know why Mr. Garrett wanted to take down the cult, and I was not sure what he gained from it except the respect of the police department. Maybe he got a get out of jail free card.

I spent one year in lock-up before being deemed normal enough to get put into a regular ward in the hospital. Most of the kids were released to foster homes or sent to live with relatives. I never understood why I didn't get to leave too. During my time in the locked ward, I had many detectives visit me, asking questions about crimes that went on that I never knew about. I tried to tell them that Mr. Garrett murdered my parents, but none of them believed me. I was told by some of my friends within the cult that Manson Sawyer was missing. He was the only one who knew everything that happened in the cult, so there was a bounty on his head. To this day, they still have not found Manson Sawyer.

I wonder now if I did not get released because of my connection to Mr. Garrett, if this was his way of tying up loose ends. I hope my story helps with our search to take Mr. Garrett down.

We will get you out of lock-up soon,

From,
Max Delbert

. . .

I woke up in the small room with Max's letter in my hand. I had fallen asleep while I read it.

I heard a soft knock on the door, and Nurse Darcy peeked her head in. She asked how I was and how the case was. I explained to her that I knew that Mr. Garrett was the common denominator in all the cases. Nurse Darcy said she could not stay and stood up, giving me a long hug, which confused me. Was I going somewhere new? Maybe I was no longer safe. Maybe Nurse Darcy was not telling the full truth.

As Darcy pulled away from the hug, she leaned in and pressed her lips to mine, but then quickly pulled away.

I couldn't believe it. Darcy had kissed me. Had she felt the same feelings between us as I had? I wanted to ask her so many questions, but before I had a chance to speak, she hurried out of the room. I knew she was not supposed to fall for the patients. She could lose her job.

13
The Ghost Hunter

I TURNED MY attention back to the letters written by my friends, pulling out the next letter, from Andrew Hadley.

Luther,

I hope they bring you back soon. It is not the same without you here. Nurse Darcy told me she is trying whatever she can to get you back.

Anyway, here is my connection to Mr. Garrett.

My parents, Thomas and Grace Hadley, were ghost hunters. They spent weeks at a time visiting different cities and towns across Canada, helping people solve their "ghost problems" while furthering their own research. They heard from this family in Rideau Ferry about the murders that were happening, and that it was always in the same house but different murders, so my parents decided to make the trip from Toronto, Ontario, down to Rideau Ferry to figure out these weird mysteries.

They started their research by interviewing all the neighbours. Many shut their doors on my parents as they thought they were crazy for wanting to know more about the murders. Most people in the town were superstitious about the house and thought it bad luck to speak about it.

Mr. Garrett learned my parents were looking around the neighbourhood, so he reached out and invited them in to check out the house. He told my parents to come after 8 o'clock in order to visit the ghosts, which were apparently in his basement. I begged for my parents to let me come. I had always found mysteries interesting and wanted to see for myself and not just read about it.

We went to Mr. Garrett's house around 8 p.m. and knocked on his door. Mr. Garrett invited us in and asked if we wanted some tea. My parents declined and told him to get right to the stories as they pulled out their notebooks.

Mr. Garrett guided us to his living room and asked us to take a seat. He started telling my parents that the ghosts would come out around nine and move items around the basement. My parents asked if they could *go down to the basement and check it out, and Mr. Garrett agreed.*

We moved down to the basement, down the creaky wooden stairs, and into a small grey windowless room. Mr. Garrett explained that the ghosts were always seen in there.

My parents questioned Mr. Garrett, asking why the ghosts were always seen there, and Mr. Garrett barked back, saying he did not know in a very scary tone. My parents continued asking about the room, what he used it for, and why he thought the ghosts showed up in his house.

Mr. Garrett started to get angry and asked me if I would go upstairs and get him his tea, and I nodded my head. As soon as I got upstairs, I heard a few loud whacks and then a scream.

I had no clue what to do. I ran back down the stairs only to see my parents' lifeless bodies lying in blood. I turned to run, but Mr. Garrett caught the collar of my shirt.

As tears rushed down my face, Mr. Garrett explained to me it was the ghosts that had killed my parents, and we needed to get out of the house now. Growing up listening to my parents about what ghosts were capable of, I knew we needed to get out of the house before we were killed too.

I followed his lead and ran behind him. I did not know where he was taking me as we ran.

We came to a police station and rushed inside. As tears poured down my face, I explained to the police officer that my parents had been murdered by ghosts and they needed to come quickly. The officer looked at me like I had grown extra heads when I explained what happened, so Mr. Garrett asked to speak to the officer alone. He said I was too upset to talk about it, and the officer agreed. The two men went into the back while another officer watched me.

They came out a few minutes later, and the officer arrested me, saying I had killed my parents. He told the other officer to put me in the car and take me to Rideau Regional Hospital.

The officer pulled me outside and placed me into his car as I screamed out, saying, "I did not kill my parents!" But the officer would not listen. I never got a trial. I was just swept under the table like a pile of dust.

The officer dropped me off to the care of the hospital, and I have not left since. I am not crazy. I should not be here. Please get me out of here and put the real murderer in.

We miss having you around, Luther. I hope you're safe.

From,
Andrew Hadley

Once I read Andrew's letter, I started to wonder how Mr. Garrett had gotten away with everything that had happened without being questioned. I needed to figure this out before anyone else got hurt. So far, I knew that, after each murder, he kept the boy child living and would at some time or another bring them to the hospital. He was never questioned by the police, so it seemed he had them in his pocket. But where was he getting this money? Did he have family money, or did he get it from these parents that he was murdering? Although he always brought or sent the boy from each murder to the hospital, the situation of each murder was different.

I was not sure that we would ever be able to solve this; each was so different, and he had already gotten away with most. Us kids were the only ones who thought any different. Would people believe a bunch of teenagers?

There had to be more to the story. I must have been missing something, so I continued on to the next letter.

14
The Bottom of the Lake

"LUTHER?" BENJAMIN STOPPED his story.

"Yes, Benjamin?" Luther responded.

"Why did you kill my father, if it was my grandfather who did all these crimes?"

"Benjamin, my dear boy, so naïve. Did you really think your father was so innocent?"

Benjamin stood up from his seat. "Luther, you keep implying this and giving no context. What else aren't you telling me?" Benjamin's voice got louder.

"Your father was at the hospital too, remember?" Luther explained.

"Yes, I remember." Benjamin huffed. "What does that have to do with anything."

"Did you know that your father was in that mental hospital for twelve years?" Luther questioned.

Benjamin fell back into his chair. "No." He couldn't deny it—couldn't argue anymore. His father had lied to him about a huge part of his life. What else had he been hiding?

"Then I suggest you keep listening to me. I promise you'll understand soon."

. . .

I knew that, if I read all the letters, I would be able to piece together enough evidence to get myself out of that room and clear my friends' names, so I pulled out the next letter.

Dear Luther,

We really miss having you at game night, but I know you will be back soon.

Here is my connection to Mr. Garrett.

I was born and raised in Perth, Ontario, and my parents, Luke and Mia Thurmond, and I were heading to Lombardy to visit my parents' friends. In order to do this, we had to take the ferry across. Everything went fine when we went over to Lombardy, but on our way back, we did not make the ferry in time. Since their friends did not have enough room for us to stay, and there was no hotel around, we had to stay the night at the ferryman's place.

Mr. Garrett invited us in, and he guided us to take a seat in his living room. He seemed nice; he made tea, and we chatted about my parents' work until it was time to go to bed. Then Mr. Garrett showed me to the room I would be staying in and bid me goodnight as he shut the door.

Everything appeared normal—until I woke up in the morning and my parents were not there.

Mr. Garrett explained that my parents had disappeared in the middle of the night, and he didn't know why. I tried to think where they would have gone, but I couldn't figure it out. They had nowhere to go.

I was so confused; I had no clue why my parents would leave me behind. Mr. Garrett asked if I had any family left, and I told him about a close family friend in Port Hope. He told me he would drive me up there.

I had not heard of the rumours about Mr. Garrett and thought he was a generally nice man, so I let him drive me to our family friend's house.

We arrived in Port Hope, and we said our goodbyes. He told me he would see me again another day, and then he left.

I spent five years living with our family friend with no word about my parents until one day when a letter showed up from the coroner in Smiths Falls, telling me they thought they had found my parents and wanted me to come in and identify them, since I was their only living relative.

The family friend drove me up to Smiths Falls, and the doctor told me a couple had been found at the bottom of the lake, and the police thought it was my parents. Since the family friend was not a relative, she was asked to leave the room and led down the hall. The doctor told me my parents had died five years ago. I pointed out that they were in the same clothes as when I'd seen them last, the night we had stayed with Mr. Garrett. The doctor said he thought my parents had gone out on their boat, hit a rock, and drowned. He told me he had examined the boat, which looked to have a large dent in the side.

On a table in the room, off to the side of the bodies, were two metal trays, which included my parents' belongings and a short rope. I asked why it was there, saying that my parents had not had a rope with them the night we stayed at Mr. Garrett's. The doctor told me that it was tied around them when they were found. He explained that it was probably floating in the water from another boat, but I knew he was lying.

I started freaking out. I yelled at him, saying, "My parents were murdered! They did not drown! Someone killed them!" The doctor yelled for help, and two orderlies, dressed in white, came running into the room and pulled me off to a different part of the hospital.

I kept yelling and screaming the whole way. The two tall men threw me in a dark grey room without windows and slid meals in on a tray. I do not know how long I spent in that room, but it was long enough to know that Mr. Garrett must have had something to do with this, and I knew the doctor was in on it.

I do not deserve to be inside this hospital. Help me get out and bring Mr. Garrett down.

I hope this letter helps,
Gabe Thurmond

I sat in that small room, and after reading Gabe's letter, I knew it was not a coincidence that we had all been sent here. I realized the hospital was in on it. If the hospital was to find out what we knew, they would keep us locked in there forever, somewhere that no one could see us, somewhere where no one could hear us, somewhere where no one would know we were alive.

Our lives were about to get a lot scarier.

15
The Harlands

"WHY HAVE YOU talked about all the boy's letters, except Louis', when he is apparently related to me?" Elizabeth questioned Luther, pulling him out of his story.

"I'm getting to your part of the story next. Now listen carefully," Luther said before he started his story again.

"No," Elizabeth said.

Both Luther and Benjamin looked at her in surprise.

"I want to know why you won't tell me about Louis," Elizabeth continued.

"What happened to listening to the story and being patient?" Benjamin mocked jokingly.

Elizabeth softened. "Fine," she said, mocking him right back.

"Thank you. Now this letter is from Louis," Luther said as he pulled another piece of paper from the folder.

. . .

I flipped to the next letter from the boys and noticed it was from Louis, who had a very similar story to mine.

Dear Luther,

I hope you're doing okay. We all miss you!

I am writing you this letter to tell you my story with Mr. Garrett.

My parents owned the Rideau Ferry store across from Mr. Garrett's house, and they were the biggest believers of the rumours about him. I started to think that some days they were making them up to scare me off.

One day, a few of my friends and I decided to break into Mr. Garrett's house when he was working on the ferry to see if the rumours were true. We climbed through an open window. I went into the house first, and I came face to face with Mr. Garrett, who I guess was on his lunch break.

I screamed and the other boys ran, leaving me behind. Mr. Garrett told me to come sit down and we would have a chat about me breaking into his house.

I was so scared he was going to start yelling at me, but he did not. He told me how lonely he was, since no one ever came to visit, and asked if I could stay for a bit to chat. I agreed as I did not want to make him mad at me. I stayed for an hour.

During this time, he told me all the fun stories he had working on a ferry and growing up here. I started to think my parents were wrong about him.

After the hour was up, I told him I needed to get home so my parents would not worry and bid him adieu. Before I walked out the door, he stopped me and asked if I would come back another day. I promised I would visit again the following week.

The next week came, and I told my parents I was headed out on our small rowboat to go fishing. I knew I would be in trouble for spending time with Mr. Garrett. My parents believed all the rumours to be true.

Instead of going to my usual fishing spot, I paddled the boat over to Mr. Garrett's for a visit.

We chatted for another hour, and when the hour was up, Mr. Garrett's phone rang. He went into the kitchen to answer it and stayed in there for about five minutes before coming back into the living room.

When he came back, he had a sad look on his face. He told me my parents had been killed, and that it was the police officer on the phone.

I was devastated and did not know what to do. Mr. Garrett told me that it was best to stay with him since I had no other family.

Mr. Garrett kept me inside for many months. He told me that my parents' killers were still out there and were looking for me. I was surprised the police never came to speak to me, but now I know that Mr. Garrett paid off the police not to question me.

Mr. Garrett and I had gotten into a good routine, but then one day he told me to me get in the car and that we were going for a drive.

We drove until we hit the town of Smiths Falls, and he eventually pulled into a long laneway with beautiful maple trees running up the sides of the lane.

We pulled up to the entrance and the sign said, "Welcome to Rideau Regional Hospital." Two orderlies dressed in white uniforms came over and grabbed me from inside the car.

I was so confused, and Mr. Garrett told me I was getting delirious, saying my parents had been murdered, and that the murderer was after me. He said I would be safer here and could get the help I needed.

And with that, he got back into his car and drove away.

I promise you, Luther, I was not delirious, and something fishy is going on.

From,
Louis Harland

. . .

Luther returned Louis' letter to the folder and looked to Elizabeth.

"But my grandparents are not dead," Elizabeth said again.

"You're right," Luther continued. "We found out years later that Mr. Garrett tricked Louis, and his parents thought that Louis had drowned in the lake that day."

"Why did my grandparents never tell me about Louis? Wouldn't he be my uncle?" Elizabeth questioned.

"Your grandparents had moved on from Louis's faked death and did not want to explain to their friends that he was alive. They always seemed to be the perfect family, with nothing to ruin their reputation until Louis came along. He was always getting into trouble with his friends, so when he disappeared, the family went back to their perfect reputation."

"Oh," Elizabeth said, looking down at the table. "I don't understand. My grandparents are wonderful. Why would they do something like this? To their own child? What else are they not telling me?"

"I am sorry, Elizabeth." Benjamin tried to comfort her by putting his hand on hers.

"Wait! Does my mother know about her brother?" Elizabeth asked in a huff of anger.

"Elizabeth, I think it's time you know that Louis is your dad, and he is alive." Luther paused. "When they found out that your mother, Maggie, who is not actually Louis's sister, or Emily and Frank's daughter—was pregnant by Louis, your grandparents decided to pretend that *she* was their daughter and shunned your father from the family. They told him he wasn't good enough to raise a daughter. His time with Mr. Garrett and the hospital had ruined him, and when you were born, they told you that your father had died before you were born. Your grandparents hated scandal, and someone staying in a mental hospital was exactly that."

"No, no! You must be wrong," Elizabeth said as she started to cry. "My father is dead, and my grandparents are good people."

"Let me finish my story, Elizabeth. You need to learn about what happened. For I am worried Louis is in trouble again."

Elizabeth nodded and motioned for Luther to continue.

. . .

I had just finished reading the letters from my newfound friends. I now knew that Mr. Garrett was somehow working alongside the hospital, which was about to make this investigation a lot harder than we thought.

16
A Sweet and Sour Lunch

I HEARD A soft knock on my door, and Nurse Darcy poked her head inside. She had a small picnic basket in her hand. "I'm sneaking you out for a couple of hours."

"How?" I asked her. "Won't we get in trouble?"

"I'm your nurse in charge today, and I thought you could use some fresh air," she told me.

She grabbed my hand and pulled me out of the room. I followed her down several flights of stairs until we came to the basement. Nurse Darcy led me down the hallway and out a door, which opened onto a beautiful green patch of grass with nobody around.

She told me to take a seat after she laid out a small patch-work quilt. I sat on the quilt, and she sat next to me as she pulled out a few sandwiches from her picnic basket. She handed me a sandwich and a bottle of pop.

"Thank you. How are the boys doing?"

She started to reply but then stopped for a moment. "Well, Luther . . . the hospital split up the boys into their own wings."

I dropped my sandwich; I was so mad I did not know where to begin.

Nurse Darcy spoke again. "Luther, we need you to solve this for all of us now. We're in this together. The hospital has been getting suspiciously large donations from an anonymous donor, and I think it's Mr. Garrett. The boys are being kept under a watchful eye, and I am putting my job on the line trying to keep myself as your nurse so you can work on this project."

I nodded my head; I knew we did not have much time to solve this. The hospital, the police, and Mr. Garrett would be closing in soon.

I looked to Darcy, who sat on the blanket with tears in her eyes. All I could think was that she was beautiful.

I moved closer to her to give her comfort. I placed my arm around her, and she rested her head on my shoulder. We sat in the silence, both too happy to move or speak. Being with Darcy made the world stand still, almost like there was nothing wrong. She made everything better.

I moved my hand to hold hers, and she looked at me and smiled. "I should take you back to your room," she told me.

"Okay." I started to help her pack up. "Just one more thing." I leaned over and kissed her. When I pulled away, both of us were blushing.

We briefly relished the moment before realizing that it was almost lunchtime, so Darcy had to get me back to my room before patients started going for lunch.

We finished cleaning up and headed back inside and up the stairs to my room.

"I will try to come back again soon. Stay safe," Darcy said as she kissed my cheek.

I waved goodbye and sat down on my bed. Of course, I knew being with her would be hard, for she was my nurse and a few years older, but after that day, I knew that I loved her.

. . .

"Luther?" Elizabeth interrupted

"Yes, dear," Luther responded.

"Was this her dress that I'm wearing now?" Elizabeth asked as she stood up in her red and white dress.

"Yes, Elizabeth, it was," Luther said as he cracked a small smile.

"Wow, I guess we would've been the same age wearing this dress. I'm eighteen now, and she was eighteen then."

"Yes, you're the same age as when Darcy wore that dress. You look like her, you know."

"Do you have a picture?" Elizabeth had become interested in Darcy and wanted to know more.

"I have one in the living room. Give me a moment," Luther said as he excused himself through the kitchen doors.

"Maybe you should become a nurse, just like Darcy." Benjamin pointed to the dress.

"I don't think I could do it," Elizabeth shyly said.

"I think you can," Benjamin poked back.

"You don't even know me."

"I know how well you have handled yourself in this situation. It's very impressive for someone who's just eighteen."

Elizabeth blushed and started to say something but was cut off by Luther, returning to the kitchen.

"Here she is," Luther said as he took a seat back at the kitchen table and handed the photo to Elizabeth.

"Wow, she is beautiful," Elizabeth said as she handed the frame to Benjamin.

"You do kind of look like her," Benjamin added as he set down the frame.

"She was a wonderful woman," Luther said with a smile.

17
My Lover's Mother

"DO YOU ESCAPE the hospital soon?" Elizabeth asked impatiently. "I want to know what happens to Darcy."

"That's what I was wondering," Benjamin added. "Also, when were you going to talk about Lucy, Mr. Garrett's first wife?"

"You mean your grandmother?" Elizabeth slid in.

"Yes, my father talked about her a bit." Benjamin smiled. "He was always happy to speak about her."

"Well, then here's the story about your grandfather's first wife, Lucy," Luther said with a saddened smile.

. . .

Lucy Miller grew up in the small town of Perth with three sisters and six brothers. A big Catholic family. When Lucy turned seventeen, her parents gave Lucy to Mr. Garrett in an arranged marriage.

She was a beautiful woman, with long, almost-black hair and very fair skin. She was about five feet tall and thin. She always had a smile on her face.

Lucy and Mr. Garrett got married that summer, and Lucy had a baby boy the following year. They named this boy Jack Garrett.

The first six months of Jack's life was great, and he was a happy baby.

Then one day Mr. Garrett decided Jack needed to go away. He got into his car, took Jack, and admitted him to Rideau Regional Hospital, the hospital for the insane.

. . .

"Wait," Benjamin said, "why did my father never tell me he was in a mental hospital?"

"He probably didn't want to relive that part of his life," Luther replied with a sigh.

"I guess it would have been hard for him, growing up in a hospital," Elizabeth suggested.

"I guess." Benjamin shrugged. "But why was he sent there?"

"Mr. Garrett told him later that his life was in danger. Some bad man had threatened to take the baby away, because Mr. Garrett had not paid his debts."

"What were his debts?" Elizabeth asked.

"Not even I know that," Luther explained. "But they were bad enough for him to send his child away to a hospital."

. . .

Lucy cried for days; she did not want to give up her only child. Just when she thought that her marriage would work out, it was on the outs again.

Lucy and Mr. Garrett tried to make their marriage work again. When Lucy was nineteen, she became pregnant and gave birth to a baby girl. They named her Darcy.

Lucy was finally happy; she had a beautiful girl, and she was loving her husband. The three of them would take short trips to their family cottage on Miller's Bay. They enjoyed the peace and quiet on the lake and loved to take the rowboat out to fish. She looked forward to the day when she could show the family cottage to Jack.

Every Saturday, Lucy snuck away to visit Jack in the hospital. She would tell him about his family and their cottage on Miller's Bay. Jack would tell her stories about his time in the hospital.

Jack always asked the same question at the end: "Mom, can I come home with you?" It broke Lucy's heart every time, until one day, when Jack was twelve, she bribed the nurse to give Jack a note with instructions and leave one of the windows unlocked so Jack could escape.

The nurse did what she was asked, and Jack escaped that night. He met Darcy's mom at the end of the driveway of the hospital. She took him to Perth where he would be safe. Then she went home.

That same night, the next town over, the hospital called Mr. Garrett's house to let him know his son was missing, and to tell his wife not come for her visit on Saturday.

Mr. Garrett slammed the phone down, grabbed a knife from the kitchen drawer, and rushed into the living room. He knew his wife had something to do with this.

Lucy was not heard from again.

Well, until Darcy found her mom, Lucy, under the floorboards.

18
The Escape Plan

ELIZABETH'S FACE FELL. "So, Mr. Garrett killed his wife because she helped their son escape from the hospital?"

"That doesn't seem believable," Benjamin puffed.

"Lucy died protecting her son's whereabouts from Mr. Garrett," Luther explained. "She loved him."

"Did Mr. Garrett ever find Jack?" Benjamin asked.

"No, but one day Jack did meet him."

"Wow," was all Elizabeth said.

"Should I continue?" Luther asked.

Elizabeth nodded, still trying to take it all in.

. . .

I learned from the boys' letters that the hospital and the police were on Mr. Garrett's side. I guessed he was paying them.

I knew the only way to stop Mr. Garrett was to stop him ourselves. We could not rely on the corrupted hospital or the police. I had learned from Nurse Darcy that the hospital was getting large donations from one Mr. Garrett. The nurses had been gossiping about these all week. Angry and confused, I felt so stupid for trusting Mr. Garrett. I'd thought he cared about me. Why would he murder these random parents? Did he hate people who were late? And then why would he send the children to a mental hospital who did not have anything wrong with them? Did he think locking us up here would keep us out of the public eye so he could get away with his crimes? I had so many questions and no answers. I wanted those answers. I needed those answers. The only way for us to get answers was to escape and ask Mr. Garrett our questions.

The first thing we needed was an escape plan.

The hospital had a pretty good security system. There was a nurse's station at the end of every wing, all main and second-floor windows had bars on them, and all doors needed a special key to open them that only the doctors had. The boys had all been moved to locked wards, which meant they could not wander the hospital as they pleased to swim or bowl, but they could have one hour of game time in the evenings. I knew Nurse Darcy had a key for my room, as well as for the locked wards, so she could give the patients their medications.

I needed a plan that could have everyone escape from their rooms at the same time. As the nurses made their rounds every hour, we would need to act fast. If we got caught, they would lock us up and throw away the key. I knew it would be best to leave at night. The night nurses were lazier and sometimes missed rounds to sleep at their desks. When we used to smoke in the games room, Louis would prop open the window to make sure we did not set off the fire alarm; that window was not locked, and there were no bars on the basement windows. They were a tight squeeze, but I knew we were all small enough to get through. The biggest key to this escape was Darcy, and I knew she would come through for us.

I pulled out my notebook and started planning. I would have Darcy leave the keys for the boys' different wards in the game room. When they got their hour of game time, they could retrieve the keys so they could leave their wards. They would need to leave their wards as soon as the nurse checked on them, so that when they left, the nurse would still be doing rounds and wouldn't see them.

Next, I would need transportation to get out of town before we were caught. I put down my pen for a moment. I had hit a dead end. *Nobody had a car. How would we get a car?* I started thinking about how everyone got there. Each of the boys had been dropped off, but Darcy had arrived in Nurse Anne's car. It suddenly dawned on me.

Nurse Darcy can ask Nurse Anne to borrow the car for the weekend and make up an excuse as to why. Maybe like Darcy wants to visit her aunt out of town? I picked the pen back up. I would have Darcy get the car and drive to the end of the driveway where we would meet her. I set my pen down again as I thought.

How can I get all this information to the boys? I decided the best idea would be to write Darcy a letter so she could share it will all the boys.

Dearest Darcy,

We need to escape tomorrow night.

Tell the boys to gather up anything we might need and to meet in the basement games room at midnight.

When you bring me lunch tomorrow, leave your key to my room under the mug on my tray. Then, after your shift tomorrow, head to the basement and make sure to unlock the window in the games room. When you head on your evening walk, crack open the basement window and put a small rock in the window frame to jam it, in case anyone tries to close it. Next, go to your apartment and gather your things. Borrow Nurse Anne's car. Tell her you want to visit your aunt on your weekend off.

Meet us at the end of the driveway in the car at 12:15. Please do not be late.

Our safety depends on you.

Yours,
Luther

When Nurse Darcy brought me my lunch that day, I slipped the note into her red and white apron pocket and gave her a nod. She pushed the note farther into her pocket to hide it from the orderly behind me and nodded. With that, she headed out of the room.

I went to bed that night with the hope that we could pull off the great escape.

19
The Great Escape

THE DAY OF the escape, Nurse Darcy brought my lunch and left the key for my door underneath the mug as planned.

Now I just needed the rest of the plan to run as smoothly.

I remember how slowly the day went by. I was so nervous as I paced back and forth in my room.

If the plan did not go smoothly, we would all be dead. If the hospital found us, we would be locked up, and they would throw away the key, leaving us for dead.

I checked the clock: 11:53.

The boys would be making their way to the game room at midnight. I knew that the guards in the wings finished their eleven o'clock rounds at 11:55. The nurses would start their rounds at 11:30, but should be past the boys' rooms by

11:55, giving the boys and myself five minutes to make it to the games room without being caught.

11:55.

It was *go* time.

I pulled out the key that Darcy had left me and unlocked my door. I peeked my head out to check if anyone was around before stepping out into the hall.

Seeing no one, I grabbed my bag, which contained my journal, and all the boys' letters.

I paused for a second to think about the great times I'd had when I first moved into the hospital, and the great people I'd met, but quickly snapped out of it. I did not have the time to reminisce.

I closed the door and headed down to the basement games room, where I hoped I would be meeting all the boys.

I was the first to arrive and checked the clock: 11:59.

I could not wait to see my friends again. It had been four weeks since I'd last seen them.

The first one through the door was Silas.

I ran to him and hugged him. "You made it!" I said to him in excitement.

"I'm so glad you're helping us escape," Silas replied.

"I'm glad you're coming with me; were going to need everyone's help with this," I said. "I'll give you a boost out the window. Head down the driveway 'til you see the red shed and hide behind it. I'll send the other boys one by one, and then we'll go meet Darcy."

Silas only nodded in reply as I boosted him high enough to crawl through the window.

Gabe was the next to arrive, quickly followed by Max and Andrew. I told each of them the same thing I'd told Silas, and then headed them toward to the shed. I sent them out one by one, not wanting us to be sitting ducks all together.

I checked the clock: 12:05.

I had ten minutes until we needed to meet Darcy, but we were still missing Louis.

I paced the room; I could not leave without my best friend.

12:07.

If he were not there by 12:10, I would have to leave him behind.

Come on, Louis.

12:10.

A tear ran down my face as I grabbed a chair and made my way toward the window. I placed the chair underneath and climbed up so I could crawl out of the window.

"Wait!"

I turned to see Louis standing behind me. I jumped off the chair and gave him a hug. "I am so glad you made it," I said to him, wiping a tear off my cheek.

"So am I. Now, let's go before we get caught," Louis said, sounding panicked. He had cut it close.

Louis and I crawled out the window and ran as fast as we could to the red shed. We met up with the boys, and I told them to follow me. We took off running to Darcy.

12:15.

Darcy was just pulling up, and we all jumped into the car as quickly as we could.

"Hit it," I said to Darcy. And with that, we sped off away from the hospital.

We had pulled off the great escape.

. . .

"Finally," both Benjamin and Elizabeth said in unison.

Luther chuckled at their impatience.

"Did you go to the police then?" Benjamin asked.

"The police were corrupt, remember, Benjamin?" Elizabeth answered for Luther.

"Then what did you do?" Benjamin persisted.

"Well, let me tell you the next part of the story," Luther said. "The hospital was just the beginning."

20
MILLER'S BAY

"LUTHER?" BENJAMIN SAID.

"Yes" Luther looked toward him.

"Why didn't Darcy want to find her brother as soon as you escaped?" Benjamin questioned.

"She thought he was dead," Elizabeth pointed out.

"Actually, I *thought* she thought he was dead, but it turned out I was wrong," Luther explained with a sigh. "Let me tell you what happened next."

. . .

We were driving away from the hospital. Everyone in the car was quiet. I had no idea where we were headed. I did not have a plan on where we were going to stay. Little did I know that Darcy had a plan.

We drove for about ten minutes before Darcy pulled down a dusty dirt road, and before long, a brown cottage appeared.

"Boys, welcome to Miller's Bay," Darcy said.

We all got out of the car and followed Darcy inside the small cottage. We were greeted by an elderly woman, and a man and woman who looked a few years older than Darcy. Darcy introduced the woman as her grandmother on her mother's side, Marilyn Miller, and the man as Jack Garrett, her brother. The other woman was Margaret, Jack's fiancée.

I was shocked.

At this time, I did not know that Jack Garrett was still alive, and I had no idea that Darcy had known where her brother was all this time. When she had told me the story about her brother in the hospital, she'd said he was dead. I don't know why she hadn't told me the truth.

"Please, make yourselves at home," Darcy's grandmother told us.

"Thank you," Louis piped up behind me.

The cottage was so warm and inviting. I was so glad that Darcy had brought us there. The boys deserved a night there before we started our next journey. They had all been in the hospital for so long.

Since it was past midnight, we decided we should get some sleep. As the cottage had three bedrooms and three pull-out couches, we each had to sleep with another person.

Darcy's grandmother woke us all up the next morning with the smell of pancakes and coffee. We all gathered around the table and ate a delicious meal as Marilyn told us about her cottages.

She had five cottages on Miller's Bay. They had been handed down through the generations, and the bay was named after her family. Each cottage was named after its colour: There was the Brown Cottage, the Pink Cottage, the Yellow Cottage, the Blue Cottage, and the Green Cottage. Each cottage had three bedrooms and a beautiful sun porch. She explained that Jack and Margaret would be given the Yellow Cottage when they got married, and that Darcy would receive the Brown Cottage when she got married. Marilyn explained how excited she was to share them with her grandchildren; the cottages were her happy place.

After Marilyn told us about the cottages, Darcy and I cleaned up from breakfast and left the boys to get to know Jack. As Darcy and I went down to the dock to talk about our next move, we discussed options for how to take Mr. Garrett down, but we both knew there was only one way. So, we agreed we would pay Mr. Garrett a visit the following day.

I enjoyed my night at the cottage. I finally had the boys back, and I was there with the girl I loved.

We played cards until all hours of the night, getting to know Jack and Margaret. Darcy was so happy to finally meet her brother in person.

I learned later that Darcy's grandmother had had someone looking for Darcy the whole time, and had tracked her down to the hospital. Darcy's grandmother would not take Jack Senior's word that both her daughter and granddaughter had passed away. Darcy had been speaking on the phone with Jack for the last few weeks. He'd told her that he'd been living in the Brown Cottage with their grandmother since their mom had helped him escape from the hospital.

Everything seemed calm at the lake, and everyone was happy. Little did we know that the hospital had noticed we were gone, and they had already called the police. We knew this would happen, but we had hoped it wouldn't.

The hospital considered us dangerous, and we were now wanted dead or alive. Of course, this was because Mr. Garrett was their biggest donor. Without the children he brought out of sight to the hospital, there would be no more money.

21
Ding Dong, the Witch is Dead

I HELPED DARCY into Jack's wooden rowboat; then I got in and pushed us off. As I started rowing toward the ferry, I could not help but notice how worried Darcy was about seeing her dad. I stopped rowing for a moment to hold her hand.

Darcy was about to see her dad for the first time in years, and I was about to confront him for everything he had done.

We pulled alongside the dock in Rideau Ferry to see Mr. Garrett's huge house. I remember smiling to myself, thinking it looked the same as it always had.

I had always felt at home there. This was the first day I felt wrong going into the house.

We did not knock but just walked through the back door that led into the kitchen. Mr. Garrett was sitting there, eating his lunch as per usual at 12:00 p.m. exactly.

As soon as we entered, Mr. Garrett stood. He walked toward Darcy, looking mad. I thought he might hit her, but he gave her a hug instead. Darcy turned white as a ghost, unsure of what to do, so she hugged him back.

He moved to me next. "I'm so glad that you've come back."

I could not take his lies anymore. He went to hug me, and I pushed him back, yelling, "I'm done with your lies!"

Mr. Garrett looked at me, smiling hauntingly. He knew I had finally figured it out. He pulled out a chair for Darcy and gestured for us to take a seat.

His dining room had not changed a bit. It was still had the ugly yellow wallpaper, white countertops, and matching white table with blue padded chairs.

He smiled. "Have you come for tea or was there something you needed?"

Darcy's expression turned to anger. "I want answers."

"*We* want answers," came a voice from behind me; it was Louis.

With him were Silas, Gabe, Max, Andrew, and Jack Garrett Junior. They had snuck in the front door, which was far enough from the kitchen for us not to hear the door open and close.

"We couldn't let you do this alone," Gabe said as he rested his hand on my shoulder.

Standing in Mr. Garrett's dining room was everyone he had hurt—at least the ones who were still living. "What do you want to know?" he asked with a smirk.

Jack was the first to speak. "Why did you send me away?"

Mr. Garrett pursed his lips for a moment. "I always wanted a son, but I owed debts to some terrifying people, who said they would take you away. So, I sent you somewhere you would be safe and paid off the hospital to keep you in a secure room."

"But then you had *me!*" Darcy said. "How come you didn't send me away too?"

"By then I had the sheriff in my pocket, and I had taken care of my debts and the people holding them over me," Mr. Garrett explained.

"Then why didn't you come back to the hospital to get me?" asked Jack Jr., his voice saddened.

"Our family was finally happy; I didn't want to disrupt the happiness with change."

Jack's face fell.

"Why didn't Mom argue?" Darcy persisted.

"Your mother was always too scared to go against me. Until one day, at least . . ." His voice trailed off.

"Mr. Garrett, why did you kill my parents?" Silas asked next.

"Because they were late." Mr. Garrett chuckled.

Silas was taken aback. We sat in silence for a moment, until Max broke it, asking his question. "Mr. Garrett, why did you want to take down the cult, and where is Manson Sawyer, the cult leader?"

"The cult added so much water traffic. It made it harder to run the ferry. And your beloved cult leader is at the bottom of the lake. I kept him around for a while, locked in my basement, until I realized he didn't know any other secret societies. Then he was no longer useful to me."

"That's it? You killed my parents, because there was too much water traffic?" Silas replied.

"Yeah, well, it also made the police like me more for taking down the cult. It gave me the chance to be on their good side, so they'd accept my bribes," Mr. Garrett answered with a shrug. "Who's next?" he asked with his hands in the air.

Andrew stepped forward. "Why did you take me to the police after you told me a ghost killed my parents?"

"So, I could frame you. I never liked you. Trying to get into everyone's business," Mr. Garrett answered easily. "Once I framed you for murder, you were locked up and out of my sight."

"You are an awful man!" Andrew yelled, jumping toward Mr. Garrett.

Gabe grabbed Andrew and held him back. "Alright, my turn," Gabe said as he kept his hold on Andrew. "Why were you so nice to me, even though you had just killed my parents?"

"I killed your parents on the night of Jack's birthday. I was thinking a lot that night about what it would've been like to have a son, and you reminded me of Jack."

Jack rolled his eyes. "You *had* a son."

Mr. Garrett just pushed past Jack's statement.

Louis went next. "Why would you tell me my parents were dead, even though they weren't?"

"I decided that I wanted a son, and so I decided you would be my son, but then you started getting nosy, asking all kinds of questions, so I sent you off to the hospital. I didn't stop thinking of you, though. That's why I kept visiting—well, until I got my own son. Helen became pregnant and gave birth to a baby boy."

"Where are Helen and her son now?" Louis asked.

"When Helen found out I had killed her husband, she took him and went to live in Calgary."

Louis didn't know what else to say.

I decided it was my turn. "Why are my brothers? Did you kill them too?"

"I always liked you, Luther. I decided to spare your brothers, but I won't tell you where they are. That's too easy," Mr. Garrett said with a smirk.

I jumped toward him, but Louis pulled me back. "He's not worth it," Louis whispered in my ear, his hand closed tight in the fabric of my shirt.

The final question was left to Darcy. "Why did you kill my mom?" she asked, afraid to hear the answer.

"Because she kept getting in the way of my plans."

Darcy couldn't take it anymore. She was so mad about the answer that she leaped across the kitchen and pulled a knife from the chopping block. Before anyone could stop her, she drove the knife into Mr. Garrett, right above his stomach, piercing his heart.

Jack ran to his father's side and checked for a pulse. Mr. Garrett was dead.

22
WEDDING BELLS

"WOW," ELIZABETH SAID, breaking the silence.

"I can't believe Darcy killed Mr. Garrett," Benjamin added as he put his hand to his head.

"Did Darcy go to jail?" Elizabeth asked, sitting up straighter.

"She must've. There were seven witnesses," Benjamin pointed out.

"Well," Luther started, "everyone was in shock. Everyone in that room hated Mr. Garrett, but we hadn't thought anyone had it in them to kill. Even for what he did to us.

"The hospital would be looking for us sooner or later, and now, with Mr. Garrett dead, we knew someone would eventually figure out it was us. We cleaned up the blood and then waited until nighttime. We wrapped the body, loaded it into the rowboat, and dumped him in the lake—just like he had done to so many of our parents.

"We decided it was best for us to split up and go our separate ways, making it harder for the hospital or police to find us. Jack, Darcy, and I decided we would stay together in Rideau Ferry to take down the hospital, and we'd let the boys know when it was safe to come back. I knew we were risking our lives, as it wasn't safe for us either, but I didn't want the hospital to get away with this. Saying goodbye to the boys was one of the hardest things I've done in my life. They were like family to me, but I knew that was even more reason to stay behind and take down the bad people at the hospital."

"Did the police ever find Mr. Garrett's body?" Benjamin questioned; his lawyer side was starting to come out.

"Sadly, yes. The next day, someone fished the body out and dropped it off outside the door of the police station, along with a note on where to find Darcy."

"Did they come to arrest Darcy?" Elizabeth worriedly asked.

"Here is what happened next," Luther said as he continued his story.

. . .

The police promptly showed up at our cottage door, demanding Darcy come out. They arrested her and took her with them to the police station, telling Jack and I that we would have to testify.

I looked to Jack; I knew he was mad that Darcy had killed their father. I also knew that he would have to have been the one who'd taken the body to the police and told them about Darcy. None of the boys would have betrayed us.

I could not betray Darcy by testifying against her.

Grandma Marilyn gave me some money to post bail for Darcy, and I went and picked her up. Marilyn was a smart lady. She knew Jack was mad at Darcy for killing their father. Darcy had gotten to have a relationship with their dad, but Jack didn't, and Darcy had just taken away his only chance to ever have a relationship with him.

I arrived at the police station and went straight to the front desk; my ball cap and sunglasses helped hide my identity. I knew it would only be a matter of time before the police figured out Darcy and I were on the run from the hospital, but in their eyes, the murder of their biggest donor was a bigger problem than a few kids escaping from the hospital.

I gave the man at the front desk an envelope of cash. He counted it, and then he released Darcy into my custody.

Darcy came running out and jumped into my arms. "Thank you for coming to get me."

"You're welcome. Let's go get in the car," I said, leading her out to the car. I ran to the passenger-side door and opened it for her. She sat down, and I closed the door behind her before moving to the driver's side and starting the car.

"Are we going back to the cottage?" she asked.

"Not just yet. We're going to go on a bit of a drive first," I told her.

"Where to?" she questioned.

"You'll see," I told her as I smiled to myself.

We drove for about fifteen minutes into the town of Perth, and before long, we arrived at the courthouse.

Darcy gave me a strange look and asked, "Why are we here?"

"Just get out of the car, and you'll see."

She did.

We stood on the sidewalk in front of the courthouse, and I reached for her hands and said, "Darcy, my love, I know you're scared, but I promise you we'll get through this together." I got down on one knee and brought out a ring. "Will you marry me? I know this is soon, but if we're married, I won't have to testify against you in court, and I know that I love you and want to be with you forever."

Darcy started to cry, nodding yes.

I pulled the ring from the box and slipped it onto her ring finger. I drew her into a hug and said with a huge smile, "Let's go get married."

We walked into the courthouse, and Jack, Margaret, and Marilyn were all there, waiting for us. I was surprised to see Jack, but I guessed that Marilyn had dragged him along.

Marilyn walked over to Darcy and gave her a hug. Marilyn had brought the veil she and her daughter Lucy had worn at their own weddings. She put it on Darcy as she shed a happy tear.

As Margaret and Marilyn helped Darcy get ready, Jack dragged me off to the side away from everyone.

"Why the hell are you helping her? She's guilty, and you marrying her means you don't have to testify against her," Jack said, shoving me.

"Mr. Garrett deserved to die after what he did to all of us," I snapped back.

"He was my father!" Jack yelled.

"And he abandoned you, sent you to a mental hospital, and killed your mother," I said with my hands in the air.

"He was still my father! Darcy is going to pay for what she did, one way or another!" Jack yelled as he stormed out.

"Margaret!" he bellowed as he walked.

Margaret quickly followed him out the door.

Darcy ran up to me. "What just happened?"

I brushed her off and said, "Jack needed to go, but everything's all right. Let's focus on us."

She nodded as she grabbed my hand and led me into the room so we could get married as her grandmother followed close behind.

"Darcy Garrett, do you take Luther Neville to be your lawfully wedded husband?" the judge asked.

"I do," Darcy said as she looked into my eyes.

"And Luther Neville, do you take Darcy Garrett to be your lawfully wedded wife?"

"I do."

"I now pronounce you husband and wife. You may now kiss the bride."

I leaned over and kissed Darcy as her grandmother threw some rice into the air. Even though it was a rushed wedding, I had never been so happy before. I had just married the love of my life.

23
The Trial

"WOW, THAT WAS so romantic," Elizabeth said, stopping the story.

"It was smart," Benjamin followed up. "Having only one witness would make the prosecution's case weaker."

"And it did," Luther explained. "When the day of the trial came, because I was now married to Darcy, I couldn't testify, so the only witness they had was Jack. That day is so much of a blur in my mind. All I could think about that day was Darcy, so I'm going to read you just a few excerpts from the court's transcript."

Luther pulled the transcript from his file folder.

. . .

Court Officer: Please stand for presiding Judge Andrews.

Judge Andrews: Everyone may be seated. Darcy Neville, how do you plead?

Emmett James: My client, Darcy Neville, pleads not guilty to all charges against her.

Judge Andrews: Very well. Does the prosecutor, Oliver Ferry, have any evidence against Ms. Neville?

Oliver Ferry: Yes, Your Honour. I would like to call my first witness, Jack Garrett.

Judge Andrews: Please state your full name for the court record.

Jack Garrett: Jack Oliver Garrett.

Judge Andrews: Do you swear to tell the whole truth, and nothing but the truth, so help you God?

Jack Garrett: I do.

Oliver Ferry: Did you see your sister, Darcy, kill your father?

Jack Garrett: Yes.

Oliver Ferry: Do you know why she killed your father?

Jack Garrett: Yes, she was angry at him for what he did to our family.

Oliver Ferry: Do you think she planned to kill your father when she went to visit him?

Jack Garrett: Yes.

Emmett James: Objection.

Judge Andrews: Denied.

...

Oliver Ferry: That will be all. Thank you.

Judge Andrews: Emmett James, your witness.

Emmett James: Was there anyone else in the room where you say your sister killed your father?

Jack Garrett: Yes, there was her husband and five of his friends.

Emmett James: Are these friends here today?

Jack Garrett: No.

Emmett James: How do we know that one of them didn't kill your father and frame your sister.

Jack Garrett: Because I don't know those people.

Emmett James: So, you're saying that you had never met those people prior to that day?

Jack Garrett: Well, no. I met them two days before that.

Emmett James: So, you're saying you had time to plan this out with them?

Jack Garrett: [silence]

Emmett James: Let the record reflect that Jack Garrett has gone quiet.

. . .

Emmett James: The defence rests.

Judge Andrews: Mr. Ferry, you may now call your next witness.

Oliver Ferry: I call Luther Neville to the stand.

Judge Andrews: Please state your name for the court record.

Luther Neville: Luther Alexander Neville.

Judge Andrews: Do you swear to tell the whole truth, and nothing but the truth, so help you God?

Luther Neville: Yes.

Oliver Ferry: Did your wife kill her father?

Luther Neville: I cannot answer that, for I cannot testify against my wife.

Judge Andrews: He is correct.

Oliver Ferry: Why did you marry Darcy Neville? Was it for love, or so you would not have to testify against her?

Emmett James: Objection, Your Honour.

Judge Andrews: Sustained.

. . .

Oliver Ferry: That will be all, then.

Judge Andrews: Defence, your witness.

Emmett James: Do you think that any of the friends who were with you the night Mr. Garrett died would be capable of murder?

Luther Neville: Yes, I suppose so.

Emmett James: Thank you. No further questions.

. . .

Judge Andrews: If there are no more witnesses, lawyers can give their final statements.

Oliver Ferry: Your Honour and the jury, Darcy Neville killed her dad to get revenge for everything he did to her and her husband. Then she married Luther Neville so that he could not testify against her.

Judge Andrews: Emmett James, your closing statement, please.

Emmett James: There is no evidence that my client, Darcy Neville, killed her father, and there is reasonable doubt since any person in that room could have killed Mr. Garrett.

Judge: There will be a recess for the jury to make their decision.

. . .

Court Officer: Please stand for presiding Judge Andrews.

Judge Andrews: You may be seated. Did the jury come to an agreement?

Jury Member: Yes, Your Honour. We find Darcy Neville . . . not guilty of first-degree murder.

Judge Andrews: Thank you. You are dismissed. The court finds that in case #365, Darcy Neville is not guilty of murder in the first-degree. . .

. . .

Luther set down the transcript and said, "As soon as they said Darcy was not guilty that day, Jack Garrett stormed out. He again said that she would pay for her crimes in a different way, someday."

"Wow, Emmett James sounds like he was a pretty good lawyer," Benjamin added as he threw up his hands.

"He was. We were quite lucky," Luther explained.

"Did Jack ever try to get his revenge?" Elizabeth asked.

"He did, and he succeeded," Luther said with a saddened tone.

24
REVENGE

"LUTHER, WHERE IS Darcy now?" Elizabeth asked.

"Is she here?" Benjamin asked as his eyes went around the room.

"Is she in this house?" Elizabeth excitedly asked.

A tear ran down Luther's cheek. "No."

"Where is she then?" Elizabeth pushed as her face fell.

"She is no longer with us."

Elizabeth looked to the ground as a tear fell down her cheek. "Oh."

Benjamin reached his hand to hers, trying to comfort her. She had grown attached to the woman whose dress she was wearing.

"Well, Elizabeth, that is the next part of my story," Luther said as he pulled her chin up.

. . .

Darcy and I were happy; Mr. Garrett was dead, and she had been found innocent of his murder.

We could finally get the justice that our friends deserved and take down the bad people at the hospital. Little did we know that Jack had other plans for us.

We returned to our lovely cottage on Miller's Bay and started to create a plan to expose the hospital for the awful things they were doing. We needed people to hear our story so we could create a group of enough people to take over the hospital.

We worried nobody would believe us. All we wanted was to save any more children from going through what I had gone through at the hospital.

We finally decided that we would go to the newspaper in the morning and tell our story for print. If the newspaper would print our story, we knew the hospital would have to shut down, or at least make some big changes by firing those who had done wrong.

I knew we would need supplies to start writing our story, and letters to others to help, so I told Darcy I would head to the small Rideau Ferry store and pick up some paper, stamps, and pens.

I bid her adieu and headed to the store.

. . .

Luther stopped his story for a moment. He had started to choke up.

Elizabeth looked to Luther with a tear in her eye. She felt sorry for him. She reached over and put a hand on his shoulder.

"Luther," she said, "what happened to Darcy? How did she die?"

Another tear ran down Luther's face as he said, "He killed her."

Elizabeth and Benjamin sat there, not knowing what to say. The three sat in silence as tears ran down Luther's face.

Finally, Luther composed himself and continued on.

. . .

I had returned home and walked into our small cottage only to find Darcy's cold, lifeless body on the floor with Jack Garrett hovering over her.

Jack turned to face me and said, "I told you she would pay for killing my father."

Tears gushing down my face, I lunged toward Jack. I was mad enough to kill him.

Jack moved just in time to avoid my deadly grip and ran from the cottage.

I yelled after him, "You'll pay for this someday, Jack Garrett." I ran to Darcy's side and picked her up in my arms. My beloved wife was dead.

I did not know what I would do next, but I knew that one day I would tell our story and make everything right, so that Darcy had died for a reason and not just revenge.

. . .

"Why did you not report Jack for killing Darcy?" Elizabeth asked.

"I knew involving the police was not what we needed to take down the hospital—"

"You killed my father because he killed your wife?" Benjamin interrupted Luther.

"I was not planning to kill your father, Benjamin; Jack had come to finish the job and kill *me,*" Luther answered.

"Why would he do that after all these years?" Benjamin huffed.

"I would imagine he was tying up loose ends, knowing that I was still gathering evidence on the hospital."

"Why should I believe that? My father was a good man," Benjamin argued.

"Sometimes people get angry," Luther calmly said.

"Is this why you wanted us to hear your story? So that, one day, the hospital can be taken down? So, Darcy didn't die for nothing?" Elizabeth pondered. "Did you ever get close to taking down the hospital?"

"Yes, I want Darcy's story and name to live on," Luther said as he wiped a tear from his eye. "I got close but could never finish it without help."

"Is that the end of the story?" Benjamin questioned.

"Yes, that's the end of my story, but it's just the start of yours," Luther finished.

25
A New Adventure

"THE START OF our story?" Elizabeth questioned.

"I could never take down the hospital. I need you two to share my story, and for once, give the hospital what they deserve," Luther finished.

Benjamin and Elizabeth sat at the table in shock, not knowing what to say.

"I need the two of you. You're my only hope, because you're the only ones who know the whole story."

Elizabeth was the first to speak. "What would my grandparents think? I would be making myself a public enemy of the hospital. They would disown me like they did my dad."

"Maybe they just need to hear the real story," Benjamin quickly added.

"Why can't the boys from the hospital share the story?" Elizabeth asked.

"The police and hospital are still looking for them. They can't ever come out of hiding until their names are cleared."

"Where is my dad?" Elizabeth pushed.

"I don't know." Luther paused. "But I do know that you can find him. If you two work together."

"I have a career as a lawyer. I can't walk away from that," Benjamin argued.

"I have my whole life ahead of me. I can't make all these enemies this young!" Elizabeth exclaimed.

"I can't do this without you two," Luther said in a saddened tone.

"Is that why you basically kidnapped us?" Benjamin snapped.

"I didn't make you stay!" Luther yelled.

Elizabeth stood. "Shut up!"

Both men looked at Elizabeth, frightened. She returned to her chair and the three sat in silence.

Elizabeth broke the silence. "I want to find my dad."

Luther looked at her with hope in his eyes. "Does that mean you will help me?"

"Yes, but I will need Benjamin's help too," she finished.

Benjamin moved in his seat. "Fine." He paused. "But only if we start with my mom. I want to know what she knows about all this. Maybe she was even in on Dad's plan to kill Luther. I need to know."

Elizabeth jumped up and gave Benjamin a hug, thanking him a million times as Luther cried a happy tear and said a little prayer for Darcy.

"I'd best get you two on your way," Luther said as he started to clean off the table. "I'll be right back."

Luther whisked out of the dining room and up the grand staircase to where he had put Benjamin's and Elizabeth's luggage. He next went into his study and reached into his filing cabinet, pulling out a small briefcase. He knew it would help the two kids. He also added the boys' letters, the court notes, a few of Darcy's personal effects, and some cash. He brought the two small suitcases and the brown-leather briefcase back down the stairs, handing them to Benjamin.

"I've put some things in the briefcase that will help you along your way," Luther added.

"Thank you," Elizabeth said as she hugged Luther.

"I hope I will get to see you clear mine and Darcy's names."

Luther shook Benjamin's hand and added, "And Benjamin, your mom should be at the Yellow Cottage."

"I guess that means we'll start our new story in Miller's Bay."

And with that, the two walked out the door of the ferryman's house to start their next adventure.

Introducing the next novel of the Ferryman's Tales:

The
Rideau
Hospital

THE FERRYMAN'S TALES

Catherine Poag

1

The Rideau Hospital

AS SOON AS they walked out the door, thunder struck and rained poured down on them.

"Elizabeth!" Benjamin yelled.

Elizabeth searched for the man who'd been standing beside her just a second ago.

"Over here!" Benjamin yelled again, waving her over to the car that Luther had given him the keys for. As the rain poured, Benjamin loaded their things into the trunk.

"Do you know where you're going?" Elizabeth yelled over the sound of rain and thunder.

Lighting lit the sky, letting Elizabeth see Benjamin for a moment.

"Yeah, I do," Benjamin said as he pushed the keys into the ignition and started the car. It came to life, and they were on their way to the Yellow Cottage.

Their first mission was to find Benjamin's mom, Margaret Garrett. Luther had told them she was staying at the Yellow Cottage on Miller's Bay. This was the cottage given to Jack and Margaret by Jack's maternal grandmother—the cottage where Benjamin used to spend his summers with his parents.

They turned down a long dirt road lined with trees. Before long, the two hit a clearing. Shortly after that, they arrived at the Yellow Cottage.

Benjamin put the car in park and got out. He went to the back of the car and pulled the luggage out from the trunk. Elizabeth followed him to the cottage's door.

The cottage was homey and smelled like fresh-baked cookies. The outside was painted white, but the trim along the windows and doors were a cheery yellow, giving it its name: the Yellow Cottage. The inside was filled with wood panelling and antique furniture; it had three bedrooms and one bathroom. It was a nice size for a cottage.

They stepped inside, and to their pleasant surprise, Margaret Garrett greeted them. She drew Benjamin into a long hug.

"I am so glad to see you," Margaret said as she let out a sigh. "I was so worried when I didn't hear from you after your flight."

"I'm glad you're okay," Benjamin replied as he drew his mom into a tighter hug. Then he pulled away and gestured to Elizabeth. "Mom, this is Elizabeth Harland."

Elizabeth reached out to shake Margaret's hand, but Margret hugged her instead.

"Harland, as in the Harlands who own the Rideau Ferry store?" Margaret questioned as she moved to the kitchen to start dinner.

"Yes, those Harlands."

"Are you Louis' daughter?" Margaret followed up.

"Yes! Do you know him?" Elizabeth got excited.

"I met him once when they all first escaped the hospital, but I'm sorry, dear, I haven't seen him since. My, you look just like him though." Margaret paused for a moment before turning to Benjamin, who was shaken to the core, realizing that she knew everything from the boys' time in the mental hospital and likely to his own father's death at the hands of his potential victim, Luther Neville.

"I thought your plane was coming in yesterday. And why is Elizabeth not at her grandparents'?"

"Elizabeth and I were on our way home from the airport, but we didn't make the ferry in time," Benjamin started. "We decided to stay the night at the ferry master Luther Neville's house for the night. Everything was going fine until Dad showed up."

"Your father was just trying to do what he thought was right." Margaret said as she set down her whisk in the kitchen and joined the two at the table, slowly sitting down. She knew this conversation would upset Benjamin.

Elizabeth continued the story, saying, "I had gone into the kitchen to help Luther with the tea when I saw Jack, your husband, lying in a pool of blood on the floor. I screamed and ran up the stairs. I thought I needed to get to safety away, from Luther . . ."

"I know, I saw you come into the kitchen." Margaret said as she hung her head.

"You were there?" Elizabeth asked.

"Yes, but not for long, I quickly escaped." She answered.

"I heard her scream," Benjamin continued the story. "I ran into the kitchen to help her, only to find Dad lying on the floor, but there was no sign of you mom. I heard another scream come from upstairs, so I turned to run up the grand staircase only to be grabbed by Luther and drugged."

"When I woke up," Elizabeth said, "Luther brought me downstairs for breakfast, leaving Benjamin in bed. I sat at his dining-room table as he served me eggs and coffee. He asked if I would like to hear a story, and I said yes. Luther started to tell me his life story, growing up in Rideau Ferry, and then living with Mr. Garrett, your husband's father. After he told me the first part of the story, he brought Benjamin down." Elizabeth stopped, letting Benjamin finish the story.

"He sat me at the dining-room table and continued speaking about how both of our families were part of it. How he'd been sent to the mental hospital by my grandfather, and then when he finally escaped, Luther's wife killed my grandfather, Mr. Garrett, and then Dad killed his wife." Benjamin stopped for a moment, not knowing how to continue.

"Why did he let you go?" Margaret started.

"Luther wants us to share his life story to clear his name and get rid of those rumours," Elizabeth sneered.

"Luther said that Dad was coming to kill him. Is that true?" Benjamin questioned.

"Yes, it is," Margaret said as she hung her head. "Your father was tying up loose ends."

"Why would you let him kill Luther, if you didn't even know the real story?" Benjamin responded.

"I *did* know the real story, but the hospital pays us a lot of money to keep quiet. How do you think we paid for your law degree, Benjamin?"

Benjamin looked shocked. "I always thought you were the good one, but maybe you're just like the rest of the Garrett family!" he yelled as he stomped off to his room.

"Elizabeth, look," Margaret started, "you should give up now before you or Benjamin end up dead too."

ABOUT THE AUTHOR

 Currently in her third year of a four-year undergrad degree at Saint Francis Xavier University, Catherine is pursuing her literary passions through editing the school newspaper and writing stories about local legends near her hometown of Smiths Falls, Ontario.

Catherine's love for writing started at a young age and grew throughout the years as she worked as a columnist for her university paper, and then moved on to be the Editor in Chief, which gave her the opportunity to freelance for the Maclean's University Guidebook.

Catherine is very involved in her community as she sat on town council as a student representative in high school. In 2017, she was a recipient of the Brooke & Brittany Henderson Award for Youth and in 2018, she received the Lieutenant Governor's Community Volunteer Award and the Lieutenant Governor's Ontario Heritage Award for Youth Achievement.